For Diane Keating

Lorraine Sharpe

Sept., 2020

CECILY

(FLOWERING, BOOK 2)

By

LORRAINE SHARPE

Cecily

(Flowering, Book 2)

By

LORRAINE SHARPE

Also by this author:

Grace Map

By Lorraine Valentin Sharpe, 2002

Dirty Feet

By Lorraine Valentin Sharpe Meyer, 2010

At Sea

By Lorraine Sharpe, 2016

Flowering

By Lorraine Sharpe, 2018

This book is dedicated to my husband George

And to his kids who have become my treasured family

Melissa, George III, Patrick, Hans and Andrew

She pulled in her horizon like a great fish net.

Pulled it from around the waist of the world

And draped it over her shoulder

So much of life was in its meshes.

Zora Neale

Hurston

Chapter 1

Cecily

1996

"OMG, My parents will kill me." That was all Cecily could think about as she walked around downtown Broken Bow, Oklahoma. She was sweating like an iced tea glass, looking surreptitiously into every shop window to catch her reflection. Was her stomach sticking out? Nope, flat as a crepe without the suzette. Maybe there was time to figure something out to satisfy her parents, but not much time before it showed.

Then she saw Rainbird come out of the hardware store jump in his dad's blue pickup and turn right, aiming to drive through town. His brown elbow was sticking out the window beating away the rhythm of something wild that he must have had on the radio and he was looking back down the street trying to move into the traffic. That's a joke. No traffic in Broken Bow. Rainbird, that's it! Rainbird will know what to do, she suddenly thought.

"Rainbird," she hollered as loud as she could to stop his truck. "Wait up, I need to talk to you."

Nicco Rainbird would know what to do. He seemed to have innate wisdom. Probably got it from his Choctaw Dad. He said that his dad sometimes went off by himself to talk to the trees and listen to the bear or the hawk when he needed peace. And boy, did she need peace.

He heard her, screeched his breaks when he saw her running after the truck. "Come on. Hop in Cecily," "What's the matter Babe?" he asked as she jumped in and flipped her blond ponytail over the back of her passenger seat. She was all sweaty, probably smelly, but he wouldn't care. She pulled down her shorts pants legs to keep her legs from burning on the hot Naugahyde seat and put the seat belt around her waist.

"Where you going?" she asked him. "Take me for a ride."

"A ride? Right now? "Why now? I was just headed home," he said.

"I need to talk to you. Please! Take me up into the mountains, to our favorite spot. It'll only take a half hour. I have to tell you something. And you can't tell your parents. You can't tell anybody what I'm going to tell you."

"Cecily, my dad will be waiting for me to help in the field. Can't we go for a ride tomorrow? I can pick you up in the morning and we'll have all day."

"By tomorrow I'll lose my nerve, gotta be today." She couldn't look at him so she just kept talking nervously, blowing bubbles with her bubble gum, tapping on the coffee cup holder. He knew something was seriously wrong. They were never nervous with each other. "I need help today, not tomorrow. Can't you call your dad and see if he can ask one of your brothers to help in the field? There's seven of you. One of your bros can help him for once. If you tell him I need you he'll let you go with me. Your dad likes me, you know. He'll give in."

"Okay, I'll try. But tell me what this is all about so I can explain to him."

"No, you can't explain to him. Just say I need you to help with something. Or make up whatever you want to say. I'll explain when we get there to our spot."

Although Nicco Rainbird was a year younger than her, hanging in his home was fun, hilarious. Cecily missed that fun in her own one-child home. She was like one of the family with the Rainbirds and Nicco, being the closest to her in age had also become the closest to her in every other way. His family treated them like twins, sat them together at the table. Put their names together, Nicco and Ceci...

Nicco pulled the truck up to the phone booth at the next corner and jumped out while Cecily fidgeted with the car radio and nibbled on the red lipstick on her lower lip. Niko came back to the truck. "Dad said it's okay. I told him you almost drowned at the pool and were so shook up you needed me to be with you for a while. Steady your nerves. He said we can start cutting hay tomorrow. He's got other stuff to do anyway."

"Why'd you tell him that? Now he'll call my dad and I'll have to explain."

"No, I told him you're okay and not to call your dad and worry him for nothing until I know more about what happened. He won't call."

They headed north into the woods at the edge of town and took a shortcut toward the overlook near the cave they often hiked to. It was cool up in these hills overlooking the Red River Valley even though it was still summer, almost September.

Nicco respected Cecily's obvious hesitation to share her problem. All the way up there he jabbered on about his family's last picnic when they all got caught in the rain. Then he started talking about his anticipation starting his freshman year in high school, about being scared. He wasn't really afraid. He was just making conversation so Cecily wouldn't have to.

When they got to their place they jumped out of the truck without a word, trudged through the thorny palms and skin-piercing thorns that were the reason their place stayed so private. They climbed up unto their own rock and sat down together looking West into the sinking sun. Nicco didn't look at Cecily.

"I'm pregnant," she burst out quietly. It was the first time she said it out loud.

"Wow! You are? I mean, what did your parents say?" he asked.

"I haven't told them yet, that's why I'm telling you." she said. "I'm afraid to tell them. What should I do? How can I tell them? 'Your angel child's been messing around and guess what. You're gonna be grandparents.'"

"You have to tell them, Cecily. They'll know what to do. Who's the father? Did you tell him yet?"

"Nope."

"Ceci, you've got to tell him."

"I'm not sure who the father is and I wouldn't tell you who it is if I did know. I'm not telling anybody. All my friends are your friends too and I don't want to ruin their lives if the word gets around."

"What do you mean you don't know who the father is? How many guys could it be? Maybe the baby's father's parents can help you. How come you don't know who it is?"

"It has to be one of the guys from the church who were on the camping trip we went on last month. I can't explain that to my parents. They won't get it.   They'll be so mad. I'll be grounded forever. Oh god, it'll be awful."

"Cecily, I don't get it either. Explain it to me. If you can explain it to me it'll be practice for how to tell them."

Before she could answer he said, puzzled, "Cecily, how could that happen on a camping trip? None of you gets to have a tent all by yourself. Did your tent mates see you doing it?"

"No, Silly. I was paired with Wanda and she got home-sick and called for her parents to come and pick her up. I told Mrs. Jordan that I didn't mind being alone for a few nights so she wouldn't have to rearrange everybody's tent space.   So, I told the whole story to Nicco, how it hap-pened.

He was shaking his head and smiling so big, but he couldn't say anything except "Really?" "You did?"

Rainbird was quiet for a while and then said, "Let's walk around for a while. It helps me think." After a few paces he asked, "Do I turn you on Cecily?"

"No, Nicco, don't be silly. If you did we wouldn't be having this conversation."

So, they walked, and walked, and stepped over fallen branches and he took her hand to help her over muddy spots and climb over three-foot-tall rocks. And he didn't say any-thing.

"It'll be okay," he finally said.

"I'm scared, for Pete's sake and you're not any help. What does, 'It'll be okay' mean? That's not what my parents will say."

So when they got back to the truck Rainbird hugged her and said "Good luck with your parents." And he drove her home as silently as they had come and she was left to come up with her own ideas about how to tell her parents, which were like nothing, nada, zero, zip, zilch.

How would she tell them? She got back home from her afternoon in the mountains with Rainbird but without an answer, not from him or the bear or trees or sky or the soaring eagle or roadrunners.

So she told her parents, kind of said it under her breath while she was washing dishes and her dad was drying, "Dad, I'm pregnant."

"You're What? How did that happen?" Then her dad called to her mom. "Evelyn, come here, talk to Cecily. She says she's pregnant!"

"You're what? Is it true?" her mom asked shocked.

"Who did this to you?" Dad asked. "When I get my hands on him…"

"It's true Dad, and you won't get your hands on him."

She was right, they did freak out. Then they had all these secret pow wows without her, like she was not supposed to know what happened, how she got pregnant. Like "pregnant" was a word you weren't supposed to say. Then they said, "You're going to stay with your Aunt Elsie in Portland, Oregon until the baby comes." They thought Broken Bow, Oklahoma, with a population of almost 4,000 people, was too small a town for someone to be pregnant in. They said, "What if everybody finds out that you're pregnant?" Daughter of Wally and Evelyn James, respected sheep raising family. How could she be pregnant. Her parents were naive. Of course, everybody'd know anyway, when she just disappeared. Where did her parents think "everybody" would think their only daughter had disappeared to right at the start of her sophomore school year?

The next bad part was them wanting to know who the father was. They put the pressure on, tried all their tricks, like saying the baby's father had a right to know. Then her mom tried, "The father must be a wonderful boy if you let him get that close to you."

The kids in the Broken Bow church and the school that Cecily attended were from four or five nearby towns as well as Broken Bow so she felt sure they couldn't just guess who the father was. She wasn't telling and she knew she had the right to refuse a DNA test since she wasn't sure who the father was, and it would require canvasing the whole class. The guys were all her friends, she wasn't going to make trouble for them. They could be expelled from school or have their lives ruined if she told, just for showing her how much they liked her.

CHAPTER 2

Waiting

1997

Cecily didn't have a chance to talk with her other friends about it before her parents put her on a train headed to Portland, Oregon. She did call Nicco to thank him for their time in the mountains. She told him that she was leaving town but said not to tell anyone else and that she'd be back next summer.

Rainbird didn't ask again about the father or lay any blame on Cecily. He said to her, "Cecily, the Great Spirit is in you, helping you give life to your baby. She will guide you and your baby. Don't be afraid. I'll be waiting for you and you'll come back safely to me next summer."

Cecily was not worried about being unable to tie her shoes or button her blouse. And she could not have imagined what it would be like to have a breaking back or a fat face. Or the good part, having big breasts and all her pimples gone. She wasn't thinking about missing school or even missing her friends. And for sure she didn't envision a scrawny little cry baby demanding all her attention. She figured she was through the worst of it already, the part about telling her parents. Now that she'd be away she could just deal with her own pregnancy her own way. Rainbird was right, but he was almost spooky. Like his dad. It was okay though. Coming from him it sounded true, like there was some spirit in her guiding her. Weird.

As much as she didn't want to leave town and stay with Aunt Elsie it turned out okay. She discovered in fact, that it was a great idea. Aunt Elsie had an important job. She was personnel director for the northwestern region of UPS and could not take much time off of work to be with Cecily, so Cecily got to stay home alone a lot. She was allowed to skip her sophomore year of school because Aunt Elsie got a private tutor for her. That way she didn't have to make all new friends at a school in Portland and explain to them why she was there.

The James' home in Broken Bow was a white frame farmhouse with two floors, the bedrooms upstairs where Cecily would not have liked climbing when she was eight months pregnant. Anyway, there was nothing to do at home in Broken Bow. What could she do with her time being pregnant here, tour the Museum of Indian History and the Railroad Museum every day?

In contrast, the house of Aunt Elsie where she stayed was a modern ranch style with four bedrooms, one of which she made her own. Cecily's room faced East, her windows welcoming the morning sun.

One room was Elsie's library. It was filled with books, floor to ceiling and even had a chestnut wooden ladder to slide along one wall so you could climb to the top to reach the high up books. Most of Aunt Elsie's books held little interest to Cecily, were way above her head, like books about accounting and business or pansy kind of novels, but she found a section on travel to be very interesting.

She discovered for herself a new goal. She would just have to become some kind of professional person that traveled as a part of her job so she wouldn't have to pay to travel. If she didn't learn anything from her tutor this year, at least she would be learning about other places not just about sheep. She pictured herself, if she got to travel sitting cross legged on the floor in Japan drinking tea and smiling till her face hurt while pronouncing "arigato gozimashta" with a bow. And she was learning about French ladies coloring their hair with henna and about floating candles down the Mekong River in Thailand. Traveling would be a wonderful life for her. She could get out of her peewee town of Broken Bow, Oklahoma as soon as she finished high school. She'd just take the baby with her. By the time she was ready to travel the baby would be old enough to go along.

And Aunt Elsie was fun, not like her mom. Elsie had never been pregnant so she got all excited watching Cecily's abdomen grow and feeling the baby kick for the first time and looking at its fetal pictures where you could see it's arms stretch and legs kick. And Elsie was lucky, she could do all this without having to look forward to her body being split open and her guts spilling out with the baby while she screamed, like Cecily knew she would have to do.

But back to the good part, every day after she discovered about the baby felt like a miracle to her. She'd lie there in bed looking at the sun shining through the bedroom window onto her stomach and think, "another person right here with me." And she'd remember Rainbird saying, "The Great Spirit will protect you and your child." Even on gloomy days, and there were plenty gloomy days in Portland, she'd cuddle up under the blanket and imagine that she was warming and comforting her baby.

Cecily's parents had a social worker, Mrs. Armstrong, sent to Aunt Elsie's to convince her to give up her baby. Mrs. Armstrong was nice but kind of old like her mom. She wore

25

tied shoes with Cuban heels and a navy sport coat and tight knee length skirt. She'd look over the top of her reading glasses and ask important things like "Who will take care of your baby while you're in school?" then write down Cecily's answers to her questions. It seemed to Cecily like the papers she had to turn in about her were more important than the actual conversation or what would happen to the baby. Armstrong said that she could find a better home for the baby than Cecily could provide. What did Armstrong know about her home?

Aunt Elsie said that the final decision would be up to Cecily. Her mom, who kept calling, was afraid, it seemed to Cecily, that she would be stuck with all the work of a new baby, like she was when Cecily was five years old and got a new puppy border collie. Cecily had promised to feed and train the dog, but Mom got stuck with the work most of the time. What did Mom think? She was five years old. Mom should have known she couldn't be reliable then. But now she was an adult, getting ready to have her own child.

* * * * *

Evelyn and Wally flew to Portland when the baby was due. They looked over the papers that Mrs. Armstrong had left. Cecily hadn't studied them thoroughly because they were too full of legal jargon. Anyway, she had decided to keep her baby, so the papers weren't important. Her mom said they were just for her to give permission for some people who wanted to adopt the baby, to come and meet her, so she could see if she liked them. Cecily felt that that would be okay. She figured they wouldn't want to come anyway when they knew she was keeping the baby. So she signed the insignificant papers to get them all off her back.

After her parents arrived it seemed like Aunt Elsie kind of changed sides on the issue of keeping the baby or giving it away. "Cecily you should think seriously about adopting out the baby, she said. "Think about how difficult it will be to have a child to take care of being a teenager and all.

"What will happen when eventually you fall in love with some guy, but the guy doesn't want to start out with someone else's baby?" she asked. "You'll have to give up the man you love, you couldn't give up the baby." "And what will the child do if you want to go out with your friends? Your friends won't like it if you always drag a crying baby with you to their parties or to the show or to dances."

Cecily had an easy answer for all of these problems. "I know my parents and friends will all love the baby so much that they'll be glad to sit for it until it's old enough to tag along

27

with me." Aunt Elsie never had a child of her own, so what does she know?

Chapter 3

Bobby

1997

The baby was born yesterday, May twenty-first. Cecily didn't let her parents or Aunt Elsie come into the delivery room. It would have been too embarrassing to have them watching her do that, push the baby out of her body, from where you go to the bathroom. Gross!

So, while they all waited in another room, beautiful, blue-eyed, bald, Bobby came out screaming. When he was born, he hollered so loud it made the nurses laugh. They said he was even louder than Cecily was when he was being born. He didn't stop crying until the nurse put him to her breast. She couldn't figure out how he knew to try to suck but he seemed to know. Cecily knew he must be very smart.

He looked right at her. She was sure he could tell that she was his mom.

She named him Bobby because it wasn't anybody else's name. The name Bobby wouldn't implicate any of her friends in her pregnancy. Anyway, she thought he looked like a Bobby to her.

Last night they took Bobby to the newborn nursery because they said that she might drop him or roll onto him If he stayed here in her bed.

Cecily thought that her parents and Aunt Elsie were very proud of her. They all said Bobby was beautiful and perfect and looked just like her.

* * * * *

This morning her nurse Marci stuck her head into Cecily's room. Marci was with her yesterday too through all her pain and when Cecily was really scared and said she couldn't do this. She held her hand and told her when to push and when to pant. She was wonderful.

"Morning Marci. Are you bringing Bobby now?" Cecily asked

Marci, short straight hair, serious eyes, wearing white scrubs with elephants and giraffes printed on them, carried

30

a small tray of medications that she was distributing. "I have to talk to you about something, Cecily," she said. "I'll be right back." When she returned she came alone, not with Bobby. She started moving efficiently around the room straitening things and not looking at Cecily. "Come over here and sit down, with me," she finally said to her.

Cecily climbed out of her bed and walked gingerly over to the two-seater couch in her room and sat down beside Marci. She tried to read Marci's face. For some reason Marci looked angry or like she was avoiding her. "What's wrong, Marci?" she asked. Cecily started to feel panicky. "Where's Bobby?" She paused and didn't get an answer. "What's wrong with Bobby?"

"That's what I have to talk to you about," Marci finally said. Marci had been left with the task of telling her that her baby was gone. Marci was under the impression that Cecily had agreed to give him up. She was angry that she had been left to tell her that he was already gone. She figured that Cecily would want to hold him again this morning before he left, meet his new parents, and say goodbye.

"Bobby left with his new adoptive parents earlier this morning. Your parents thought it would be better for you if you didn't see him again so they didn't tell you yesterday exactly when to expect the new parents to come for him. They wanted to save you from the pain of saying goodbye."

Cecily shook her head and cried out loudly in a panic. "No, that's some kind of mistake. I'm not giving him away,"

Marci was confused. Suddenly it dawned on her for the first time, that Cecily thought she would be taking Bobby home. She was horrified to be the one left to break the news that Cecily wasn't keeping her baby at all.

"Mrs. Armstrong said that you agreed to give him up." Marci waited for some sign of recognition from Cecily. "The people who came for him had all the signed papers, she said. "I checked the papers and Mrs. Armstrong was here with the new parents when they came. They seemed to be very nice. I'm sure they'll take good care of him for you." Marci was scrambling for words to calm down this horrible situation that she had been placed in unprepared. She would never have accepted that responsibility that belonged to Cecily's parents.

"No, I didn't agree to that. I just agreed to talk with these people who were interested in him. I have it all figured out now, how I can take care of the baby and finish school too. It won't be too much trouble for my parents. My friends will help with Bobby too when I can't be there with him."

Marci tried to hug her to comfort her but Cecily would have none of it and pulled away.

"I'm so sorry," Marci said

"You don't mean it. You're joshing me. He's not actually already gone."
Silent confusion bounced back and forth between Cecily and Marci.

"Oh my god, you do mean it...I'll call my mom. She'll tell you what I signed. She knows I'm keeping my baby. They can't have Bobby. You have to stop those people fast, before they get too far away." Cecily was in a panic.

She grabbed the phone and dialed, stumbling over the numbers with her shaking fingers. The phone at her parents' hotel rang and rang. "No one is answering so I know they're on the way to the hospital."

Then she tried Aunt Elsie's phone. Elsie answered on the first ring like she was waiting for the call. "Aunt Elsie, the nurse said my baby is gone. You have to do something."

"Oh, my dear," Elsie said to her. "I'm sure your parents are on their way to the hospital now. I'll be there just as soon as I can." Elsie had insisted that her sister Evelyn, and Wally talk with Cecily before she arrive at the hospital. She strongly disagreed with the way they were handling this situation, but Cecily was their daughter and Elsie did not want to be in the middle of it.

Marci just stayed seated in her room while the phone calls were made, wanting to be available for whatever she might need.

The tears were burning Cecily's face when her parents pushed open her hospital room door. She jumped up and ran to the door as quickly as she could. Her mom put her arms around her but looked away, at her dad.

"Something terrible has happened," Cecily cried to her. "You have to do something. Bobby is gone. Those people who were supposed to come to meet me...they took Bobby. There was some mistake. The nurse thought I was giving him up. Hurry, call those people for me."

Evelyn and Wally looked helplessly at each other. Cecily suddenly realized that there was no urgency in her mom's response to this crisis, only sadness and resignation. "It will be okay," Mom said. "Your son will have a good home." Evelyn eyes were saying to Wally, "Some help here please." Dad, even more helpless, patted Cecily's shoulder and said, "There, there."

When she looked from Mom to Dad and back again, she suddenly realized the truth of the matter. "You knew he was being taken from me. You planned this. You tricked me.

It's your fault that Bobby's gone." It only took that moment for her to know, there was no way that she could count on her parents to help her get Bobby back. She fell onto the bed, wailing so deeply that it felt like her wail was coming from the center of the earth.

Trying to make her daughter hear her over her convulsive sobs, Evelyn padded Cecily and said to her, "Our car is here and loaded. We'll take you home to Broken Bow now. You don't have to go back to Elsie's. It's time for you to heal and to be young again."

"No way. You don't get it do you?" Cecily cried to her mom. Then she motioned to Marci. "Please call my aunt" she whimpered," and ask her to come for me at discharge time. If she can't come, I'll need a taxi. I'm not going back with my parents. They can't force me. I'm staying in Portland until I find Bobby."

* * * * *

Elsie looked like an older sister to Cecily, more than like a younger sister of Evelyn. She was taller and more slender than Evelyn and dressed younger. This morning she wore mid-thigh denim shorts, a yellow and white striped sweatshirt with a big University of Oregon logo on the front and Nike running shoes, looking like she had run all the way here from her home. Her still-blond and still-wet hair was pulled up in a ponytail like Cecily's.

Evelyn, with bloodshot eyes, turned to the door when Elsie pushed it open. "Elsie, thank God you're here." Then a long silent pause as they all looked at each other for an answer. "Do you think you will be able to keep Cecily with you a little longer?" Evelyn finally ventured.

"I would be happy to take you home with me, Cecily," she said, but let's be sure that is the best thing for you to do. I can take a few days off of work so I can be with you until this is settled."

"It doesn't matter what anybody else thinks is the best for me. I'm not going home," Cecily said. "I just want to stay until I find Bobby," she added, obviously addressing herself only to Elsie, "then I'll go home to my parents."

Finally, Wally suggested, "Cecily, why don't you stay with Elsie tonight to give us all time to think about this and talk it over before we leave. You must be very tired. Your mom and I will stay at the hotel again to give you time to think about your future without our interference. Aunt Elsie will help you and you can call us when you're ready to talk with us."

Wally was so cool headed, Evelyn thought. Of course, a 1996 teenage perspective of this was different than the perspective of her "great generation" parents. Cecily and Elsie nodded agreement with the plan.

Both parents hugged Cecily before they left her room. Evelyn wrapped her arms tightly around her daughter whose arms hung limply at her side. Evelyn could only say, "I love you," and she said it with all of her broken heart. Then Wally hugging Cecily tightly said, "Whatever happens next, I will always love you my baby, more than my own life. You will always be welcome in our home no matter what you decide to do now."

With silent looks of gratitude both parents hugged Elsie briefly and said, "We'll see you tomorrow," and left the room.

* * * * *

Tomorrow turned into four days later. Wally and Evelyn hung on every moment, waiting. They ordered some meals brought to their room so that they would not miss the call when it came. They took turns leaving their room and when they did they stopped at the front desk to find out if any messages had been left for them. Wally lay awake at night. When Evelyn moved, he asked, "you awake?"

"Yes, are you?"

"I'll make coffee."

"Okay."

By the third day they were exhausted.

When Elsie called, she said that Cecily was so tired she slept most of the time and when awake ate a little and seemed bewildered. She wasn't ready for this conversation. That would feel to her like defeat.

Wally and Evelyn were experiencing grief just as Cecily was, knowing that they had lost their daughter's trust.

"Wally, did I do the right thing? I never intended to deceive her. I was trying to ease her into the inevitable decision she would have to make. Her life would be so changed, so limited with a child to raise. I understand that she can't see that now, so I thought I was helping by taking away her responsibility and the pain of making that decision."

"Evelyn her life is already so changed whatever decision she makes. At fifteen years of age her life changed in a way that can never be reversed. It is not in our power to save her from adulthood now. She has lived through pregnancy and childbirth and the ecstatic experience of seeing her own child for the first time. You remember what that was like! We also know what it's like to lose a child.

"But yes, you did do the right thing. You always try your best to do what is right for others, and I will always support you."

"But Wally...

"She's so young."

"Evelyn, Cecily has made decisions based on her own generous nature, based on what you and I have nurtured for sixteen years. The love we have given her and all that we have taught her will stand her in good stead in a future that we cannot control. She decided not to abort her baby. She has not blamed anyone else for her pregnancy. She refused steadfastly to blame or expose the boy who is the baby's father. These were all decisions that speak to her integrity.

"She would have loved her son, but with a child's understanding of the burdens it would impose on her and her son and us. One day both she and her son will be grateful for the good home that will be given to him. But for now, we have to understand that "one day" may be a way off. We cannot expect gratitude from her, we can only be there for her as she struggles with her decisions."

"Wally, do you think we should try to reverse our decision and see if we can get the baby back?"

"No, Evelyn. We would only create more devastation. Both Cecily and Bobby would be back to the more limited futures that we were trying to avert. "The new adoptive parents would be crushed by the loss of their baby son. No, our decision was right. It was only that we failed to help Cecily make that decision too. That's what was wrong."

"Maybe we should have kept her home during her pregnancy."

"Perhaps, but that's past," Wally said. What we did seemed like the best decision at the time. It doesn't help to second guess ourselves now."

"Cecily is not ours, is she. She is her own person. We cannot dream for her."

On May twenty-sixth Elsie finally called. "Evelyn Cecily is willing to talk with you now. Of course the outcome of all this is up to you and her, but just to let you know, if you think it is for the best, I will be happy to keep Cecily here for a while longer."

The visit between Cecily and her parents was cool and brief. Cecily refused adamantly to return to Broken Bow without Bobby although she had done nothing yet to see if she could find him or trace his new parents, or the agency who handled the adoption.

She agreed that, if she was still in Portland at the beginning of the new school year, she would enroll in high school there.

"Cecily you are always welcome to live with me, but I will not plan to help you retrieve Bobby," Elsie said. "I need you to understand that I do not think it would be good for Bobby to be taken from a good home just to be raised by a teenager, no matter how much that teenager loves him."

"I don't need you Aunt Elsie," Cecily said. "I know you're busy and you have a job. I can take care of things myself. I'm an adult now, you know."

When school started in September and Cecily enrolled in high school in Portland, Evelyn started quietly to put her things away. Wally stopped saying, "When Cecily gets home..." Both of them knew, that deep in the heart of the other was the hope for that "one day" to arrive when Cecily could understand and come home.

Chapter 4

Evelyn and Wally James

1950

Evelyn Hemlock, the oldest of seven children, grew up too young when, at five years of age she was expected to help her mother with her two younger siblings while her father went off to the Korean war. She would sit on the day bed and hold the baby and sing to him until he went to sleep while she watched her mother iron sheets for their own and others' households, washed diapers and handkerchiefs, stretched curtains and help the elderly neighbor next door. Together her mom and five-year-old, obedient, proud little Evelyn earned a livelihood for the family of four until Dad came home.

When dad did come home from Korea, more siblings started arriving. Evelyn went to the local school in Norman, Oklahoma. She was industrious but made few friends, not that she was unfriendly. She secretly longed for intimacy, for a buddy, but was unable to initiate peer relationships. She usually sat alone on the school bus and went straight home after school. Her classmates thought of her as matronly with her mousy brown braided hair and laced up black oxfords and cotton dresses a little too loose and a little too long.

One day shortly after her youngest sister Elsie was born, while Evelyn was trying hard to hush the crying teething baby, mother came home and unloaded five heavy grocery bags from the cart that she pulled when she walked to the store. She flopped down onto the nearest kitchen chair and said to her thirteen-year-old daughter, without any trepidation in her voice, "Evelyn, I got myself a job. I'm going to be a receptionist in Doctor Keating's office. You're old enough now to take care of the babies and you seem to love doing it."

Evelyn became a virtual mother to her siblings. She did love doing it, but she had never had a chance to be a teenager. Evelyn didn't even know how to say 'no', let alone rebel.

Elsie the youngest, was the family wild one. In the 1970s it was Evelyn who sat up worrying and waiting for Elsie to come home from a date.

Elsie would waltz in the front door after a kiss from her date under the porch light always a little past her curfew and Evelyn would feel a twinge of jealousy. Yet somehow, Evelyn didn't wield quite the authority that a parent would have.

One-by-one the other children left home for school in other parts or for marriage. Evelyn kept up the home front for her parents. She often had employment in town, clerking in the Woolworth store, substituting for her mother as receptionist, or helping out at Ace Hardware. She also worked on neighbors' farms, helping to harvest crops in summer and fall and sometimes babysitting. Evelyn often went to her town's hoedowns and swung her hips happily to square dances or round dances with the town folk but was almost never asked to partner anyone in the slow dances like waltzes or two-steps. The young men she knew in town probably assumed that she wasn't interested in them.

Then one year at the Halloween Hoedown an unfamiliar gentleman appeared. He was wearing boots, denim overalls, a red shirt that almost matched his auburn neatly cut hair, beard and mustache and had nice teeth and a bright open-faced smile. He kept watching Evelyn during the first hour of the dance.

Evelyn felt nervous when he finally approached her. Holding out his hand to her he said, "Beautiful lady, would you be willing to dance with a goat of a man like me?"

Surprised, abashed, Evelyn reached out her hand to his. She couldn't speak. Neither of them spoke any words during that first dance. Wally held her firmly and led the waltz step boldly. He seemed confident, like he really wanted to be with her. And best of all, he didn't smell of smoke or alcohol. She felt like she wanted to stay in his arms for a long time.

This man would not disappear as quickly as he had appeared. Suddenly, what she had worn that night mattered to her. Here in his arms, why was she thinking of her clothes and looks? She was glad she had dressed her best that night, not in some silly rag doll costume as her mother had suggested. She wore her French blue sweater set and knee length leather western style A-line skirt and her brown leather boots with two-inch heels. She had pulled her now thick, brown silky hair back away from her face with her favorite flowered combs. She had worn light eye make-up to accent her blue eyes and hardly any lipstick or rouge.

"I'm here in Broken Bow with my uncle," Wally told her. He's making some kind of business deal having something to do with his sheep, but I'm not involved with the business. I just came along for something to do. I have time to waste. I'd sure like to waste my time with you this week."

"Courting Evelyn will be the best waste of time I will ever spend," he bragged to his uncle.

"Evelyn, I'll come fetch you in the morning if you tell me where you live," Wally pleaded when they were parting that night.

"Well, where would we go in the morning?" she asked.

"Doesn't matter to me at all. You decide. We can just walk around town if you're not embarrassed to be with me," he said.

"Embarrassed? Why I'd be so proud," she said.

So that's what they did. The two of them spent most of the next three days walking through town, meeting family and neighbors including three of her siblings who still lived in Norman with their families and sitting on their porch swings.

By the end of the whirlwind, at least it felt that way to Evelyn, sitting on her brother Ivan's front porch, Wally asked, "Evelyn, ride with me and my uncle to Broken Bow, will you?

I want you to see Uncle Ben's sheep ranch and all. Maybe someday we could have one like his."

"Did he really say that? she asked Ivan. "We? Like it was a done deal that they were now, 'we'? Evelyn's heartbeat fast, she couldn't erase her smile. She had no idea what being in love was supposed to feel like but this had to be it. One dance in one instant changed her whole life.

Evelyn and Wally were married within four months. They immediately purchased six acres of land in Broken Bow from Wally's uncle to begin their own sheep ranch.

"Uncle Ben, you have to come over here and teach us how to rear these blessed sheep," She said to Ben soon afterwords. "I know what to do when a baby cries but sheep? Wally says I'm not to cuddle these little lambs when they're making a racket. It's their mom's job. But I can't resist them. What should I do?"

"I think you need a little human," Uncle Ben said.

But, although they both loved their land, their little house with blue and white gingham curtains, their six starter-sheep and each other, they didn't expect to have children. Evelyn was thirty-six and Wally, forty-four when they were married, a little older than any of their siblings had been when starting families. Now it would be just her and Wally, child rearing was behind her.

But by the end of 1980 their first year of marriage they were rocking the cradle of the most beautiful little girl ever born. They named her Cecily Wallie for Wally's sake because they didn't expect to be blessed with more children. But they tried. Evelyn didn't want Cecily to be an only child and Wally agreed that a sibling would be good for Cecily, the best gift they could give to their first child.

And then Evelyn became pregnant for a second time. When she passed four months the doctor saying everything looked fine, Evelyn started cautiously to fold and sort tiny baby clothes left behind by Cecily. Wally prepared a junior bed for Cecily so she could make room in the crib for the baby, a little brother, he hoped secretly.

"I don't know how I ever did without you and your mother in my life," he told Cecily.

"You have sheep," she answered, and he grabbed and hugged her.

"Yes, I have sheep," he croaked.

When Evelyn and Wally's son Jacob was born, he too looked like a perfect child. Then, on the fifth morning after his birth, still in the hospital where he was born, the nurse checking on him found him dead in his nursery bed. The term SIDS was new at that time but infant death with unknown cause was not. And the devastation that this loss caused the parents left a hole in their lives and their hearts of a shape that no one else could fill.

Jacob had been examined by a pediatrician and proclaimed healthy. Jacob had caused them to smile when they looked into his big blue eyes. Jacob had a big sister waiting excitedly for him to come home. Jacob had a nickname, Jake. He was a little boy who made gurgling sounds and grabbed their little fingers with his fist. Jake made Walter's step bounce as he came to the hospital the four mornings after his birth.

With the loss of Jake, they also lost hope of a future sibling for Cecily. They could not go through another hopeful pregnancy. They could not experience the exhilaration of new life only to have the life gone so instantly and so totally.

Evelyn and Wally were determined that Cecily would have plenty opportunities to make close friends and that her friends would always be welcome in their home. They enrolled her in day care, in 4H, in every healthy social setting that they could find in their small town. Cecily was their tomboy by her choice, not theirs. She was more at home out in the sheep pen in her denim overalls than in church or in social settings in a pink dress and ribboned hair.

Wally one day showed Cecily the grave of her brother under the willow tree. "Mama says my brother is with God," Cecily said.

"Yes honey, he's with God, but so are you and me and Mama. But some of us get to have longer lives than others on this beautiful earth. We don't have to die to be with God."

By the time Cecily was four years old the grave seemed to her to be just a part of the landscape. Her parents, though they wanted her to know about her brother, didn't want her to understand and experience their pain. Cecily made friends easily and liked bringing new acquaintances home to meet her parents and her male dog that she named Daisy Jane, and her sheep.

Chapter 5

Aubrey Gentile

1985

"Hey Aubrey, come on, we're waiting for you." Five-year-old Cecily called out from in front of Aubrey's house. She was hanging on to Wally, her arms almost reaching all the way around Wally now."

Aubrey's mom impatiently pushed him forward. "Hurry up Aubrey. Don't keep Mr. James waiting every day or I'll have to drive you to day care in my truck."

Little Aubrey, shorts exposing scabs and band aids on both knees fumbled out the doorway to the tractor and climbed up to his special spot in front of Wally. "I'm sorry Mr. James. Mama said I can't come with you anymore cause I'm always late," he said.

"I'll talk to your mama Aubrey. I'm sure she'll let you ride with me and Ceci. Come on now, let's go."

* * * * *

Three years later they did switch to the truck so that they could take the lamb that they were sharing for the 4H Club project along with them for the ride.

"My dad says we can't name our lamb because he's not a pet," Cecily told Aubrey.

"I won't tell," he said. "You and me will have our own special name for him. We can call him Billy."

They alternated weeks with Billy. One week, he would live at Cecily's and she would be responsible for him. Then Mr. Gentile would bring Aubrey to the sheep ranch and they'd have lessons about sheep together. Then the Gentiles would drive home with Billy and Aubrey would be responsible for him the next week.

They learned together to be responsible, to protect Billy, to feed him, to give him salt and to shear him. They learned to move him from paddock to paddock when the grasses were too short because of the goats' good appetites. They learned the difference between a ram, a ewe and a lamb.

Ten-year-old Cecily and Aubrey stood watching Billy in the coral with big eyes and open mouths. They had witnessed animal life all of their lives but had not pictured Billy out there with the ewes. "Go Billy," Aubrey yelled when he saw Billy climb on the ewe. Cecily said, "Yuck."

Neither of them dared look at each other as they stood there, but Aubrey slipped his hand over hers. They stood for a minute, entire brains focused on those hands and finally Aubrey said, "Can I kiss you. Cecily?"

Cecily tipped her head to one side, her blond ponytail flipping across to her shoulder. Then she closed her eyes and puckered up, silently inviting him into her space. Aubrey leaned over to her and quickly placed one on her lips. Then she opened her eyes and both of them grinned ear to ear at each other.

Cecily was coy with Aubrey after that. There was something about how her blue eyes smiled even when her mouth did not. Neither she nor Aubrey even noticed that she was white, and he was black. Nor did she notice that their lamb was white with black spots. That didn't matter to her any more than it mattered that her border collie was male when she named him "Daisy Jane."

The day of their kiss was the day Aubrey broke his foot. A minute after the kiss, both of them still tingling with excitement, Cecily interrupted with, "I'll race you to the barn." They both took off, climbed the ladder to the top of the hay stack, she jumped first, then after her jump she heard him scream.

"Oh no Aubrey."

"Come help me," he yelled. "I can't walk. Maybe it's my punishment for kissing you."

"Don't be silly, Aubrey. You don't get punishment for kissing. You just get tingles. But come on, I'll get you home."

Cecily pulled Aubrey up on his one foot and crutched his other side while he hopped all the way home.

It would seem that this would have been the beginning of a courtship for the two of them but as it turned out, it was not. Both of them were old enough now that their help was needed on their parents' farms, Cecily with the sheep and Aubrey with the corn and vegetables. They began to hang out more with their same gender peers in school, watching each other at a distance with curiosity and hidden desire. Aubrey could pick Cecily out from a distance, standing around with her girlfriends, by the tip of her head and by her gracefulness. And then one day she was gone from the town and he didn't know why, though there were rumors.

Aubrey's broken ankle was fortuitous. It was his experience in the emergency room with the nurses and hospital staff who treated him like an adult, explaining their procedures, were gentle with him when he was in pain and calmed his fear, that beckoned him to his life's work. After high school he left Broken Bow to enroll at the University of Tulsa and earn a bachelor's degree in nursing.

Chapter 6

Graduation

1999

Evelyn turned the eggs over in the bacon grease absent mindedly, forgetting that Wally preferred sunny side up. Wally knew that glazed over look on her face. "What is it babe?"

"Wally, I couldn't sleep last night. I kept thinking of Cecily, ready to graduate from high school and already gone from us for two years. I wish we could help her. But how? We can't force her to come home."

"No, we can't force her," Wally said sadly.

It was almost like their thoughts and conversation had been heard for thousands of miles, through the clouds or airwaves or something. The phone rang just as Evelyn was cleaning up the dishes from breakfast and Wally had retired to his desk.

"Evelyn, this is Elsie. I'm calling to invite you to Cecily's high school graduation."

Evelyn was elated but sad and confused all at the same time.

How did this happen? How did their baby enter adulthood without them being allowed to enjoy her? Cecily was not a wild child, never had been. Her pregnancy was a one season event Evelyn was sure. And all of their lives had been stopped dead in their tracks in the moment that she conceived a child.

"Does Cecily know you are calling?" Evelyn asked.

"No not yet, but you must come. Maybe seeing you there to support her will help her decide to return home," Elsie said.

"Elsie, haven't we learned yet? Cecily is making her own decisions especially now that she's eighteen. Please ask her to invite us. Of course, we want to be there, but we will not surprise her. She has to want us to come."

The next day Cecily called. "Mom, Aunt Elsie told me she invited you to my graduation. Sure, you can come if you want to, and you can stay here at Elsie's. But I won't have much time to spend with you. I'm starting a new job a few days after graduation." Then she paused awkwardly. "I have to go now. I'll see you next week." Cecily hung up the phone.

Evelyn was doing a little tango kind of step as she glided onto the closed-in back porch that overlooked the cornfields and their barn. Wally was there in his bib overalls as usual sitting at his desk pen in hand and quiet in thought. He looked up at Evelyn. "And what brings you bouncing in here my dear bride?" he asked.

"You'll never guess who I just spoke with," she answered.

"Jack Benny?"

"You're favorite, and only shepherdess," she answered.

"Cecily?"

"You bet. She's graduating next Friday, and we are invited. Get on that phone right now and order our plane tickets to Portland."

Details Evelyn. Details. How did she sound? … Is she excited? … Is she coming home?"

"Wally dear, we can always hope. She said she's starting a new job and won't have much time so don't count on bringing her home. She was very brief on the phone. But we're invited…and we can stay with Elsie where Cecily will be. Maybe we will have enough time to learn more about her, and just maybe, seeing us will make her homesick and she'll want to come home."

Evelyn continued, "I have to go now and see if I have everything I need to bring on the trip. I'll start packing my bags. We must figure out what to buy for her."

"Now look who's getting too excited," Wally teased.

That evening and all the coming week they mused together on their upcoming visit with Cecily, their first in two years. Evelyn pictured her finally back in their home, sitting sideways in the living room armchair, legs over one arm, flipping through a magazine. Wally could just see her helping her mom around the kitchen. They would manage to be whomever she wanted them to be on this trip. They'd talk about her new friends and the old ones. If she was ready, they'd even talk about her pregnancy and about her son. They'd let her take the lead.

They decided to give her gift certificates for Troutman's Emporium since they no longer knew her size or taste in clothes and didn't know what needs she would have in school or work. They wrapped up boxes holding some of her favorite childhood things, a stuffed lamb, a truck, a dollhouse and dollhouse furniture, and put a gift certificate in each box. This way she would have something to open and still have the money she would need. Wally felt that seeing and holding these familiar things would help her feel kindly toward them and toward her home again.

* * * * *

Cecily couldn't wait until she had that diploma in hand. She had never felt comfortable with her junior and then senior high school classmates. She was much too grown up for them. While they were wearing training bras, she had been busy expressing and crying over spilt breast milk. They were busy comparing colors and lengths of their fingernails with embedded rhinestones and flirting with the boys. She on the other hand had been through pregnancy, labor and delivery, had left home and had tried to earn and save a little money to support herself. She would be responsible for herself after she was finished with school. Her classmates were a bore.

More important than any of that, she had been unable to find her son. She had started with Mrs. Armstrong, the social worker who arranged "the kidnapping". She had first tried pleading and then demanding to know how to find Bobby. Mrs. Armstrong tried to convince her that the adoption was best for everybody, especially her son. Then when Cecily would not give up she just said that it was a closed case and that even she did not know where Bobby was. Cecily tried everyone she could think of to help her, her school counselor, the nearby office of the Lutheran Social

Services, even tried the minister of the local church who suggested praying. She knew that God, if there is one, would not override the decisions that the responsible people made. God was on their side not hers. So, prayer was a bust.

Cecily was defeated. Sometimes her stomach felt like it contained a big boulder. The boulder and lots of milkshakes kept her from losing weight so nobody noticed that she wasn't eating. Elsie wasn't home for dinner very often. Her work as personnel manager of the Northwestern States District of UPS kept her at work late on most days. When she got home from work Cecily usually just said she had already eaten and had homework to do. Eventually Cecily got a job at McDonald's on the weekends so, the milkshakes were free, and she and Aunt Elsie saw even less of each other.

Cecily's perfect small figure, blond hair, bright blue eyes and the quiet smile that warmed others, belied the chill that she felt when thinking of her next step in life. She wanted to be away from Portland, from Elsie, from family eyes. She had found a clerk job in Seaside, Oregon where she knew no one. She would still be in Oregon which was important in case Bobby or his parents tried to find her. She would continue her schooling while she worked so that eventually she could make something of herself. Maybe travel the world once her Bobby was found.

* * * * *

As Wally and Evelyn watched Cecily at her high school graduation, walk across the stage to accept her diploma, they felt so proud but yet they were almost startled to see the confidence of her walk. Her five feet five looked tall to them, straight, graceful, mature. Her childhood was obviously over. As they watched her they both wept.

The morning after her graduation Evelyn and Wally drove Cecily to the train station. The three walked together alongside the train while it emitted scraping noise and steam bursts. Scurrying conductors helped them find Cecily's coach car with the sign "Seaside" in the window. They boarded the train with her to help her with her luggage including all of their gifts. Wally lifted the luggage into place then hugged her and said to her, "my baby, we only want you to be happy."

"The last time I can remember being completely happy was the day that Bobby was born," Cecily said coolly.

It wasn't right for an eighteen-year-old child. She should always be completely happy, Evelyn thought, but the right words wouldn't come to her. "Please let us know when you get settled safely," Evelyn said as she hugged Cecily.

"I will," Cecily said. "I'll call when I get there."

"And we want to know all about your new job and how it goes finding a school. And let us know if you need anything. We'd love to help you get settled. And tell us about your new apartment when you find one...or your roommates."

Then they all three stood silently, not knowing how to step away from each other, then Cecily sat down in her assigned seat and said "Bye," so that her parents could feel free to turn and walk away. The hardest part for all of them was when Cecily's parents stood outside the train window and waved intermittently while Cecily sat inside. They tried to motion their thoughts, none of them able to be heard through the train window. Despite the awkwardness, Evelyn and Wally just could not leave until the train pulled away.

And when it did and the train and was out of their sight, Cecily wept.

Chapter 7

Aubrey

2002

Aubrey liked the last row of seats in a classroom. From there he could survey the other students, their reaction to the professor, he could tell if he was on track with the rest of the students or ahead or behind. He could disappear if he felt self-conscious or leave if the class was boring.

He climbed up to the back row of seats on this first day of his anthropology class.

"Why are you enrolling in Anthropology?" the student counselor of Lewis and Clark College had asked him, when he tried to gain admission to an already overfilled course. Aubrey expected that full disclosure would exclude him from the course but honesty, full disclosure was a part of his psyche. He couldn't do otherwise. "To be honest, it's just on a lark," he answered. I don't need a degree. I already have a

Master's from UCLA and I'm working for the Public Health Department of Portland. "I'm fascinated by Anthropology and I figure that someplace along the line it will help the Public Health Department.

"How many of you are taking this course as part of a degree requirement?" Professor Dawes was getting a portrait of his classroom and so was Aubrey. Almost all the hands went up. "Anybody here just because you think this subject is fun or interesting?" Aubrey put his hand up tentatively. There was only one other in the whole forty student classroom that wasn't afraid to admit it. The other one was a blond with a ponytail way up front. I think I have to meet that woman Aubrey thought. As the class proceeded, he couldn't take his eyes off of her. Something about the way she flipped her head, the ponytail swatting her chin, reminded him of a little blond girl in his past. She looked vivacious and interesting and the truth was, "flirt-worthy."

The two-hour class was over, and students began shuffling their papers and gathering their books. Aubrey edged his way down toward the front of the room.

"Pardon me, Miss," he waited for her to look up.

She looked up directly into his eyes. "Aubrey?"

"Cecily?"

"Is it really you?"

"It can't be. Another student from Broken Bow here in Portland?"

"I can't believe it."

"What are you doing here?"

"Can I hug you?"

"Of course."

They grabbed one another tightly…and long.

"Hey, everybody's looking at us"

"Can we go someplace and talk?"

"Of course, cafe' downstairs?"

Aubrey picked up Cecily's books and waited for her to lead toward the doorway.

* * * * *

"Hey, you go first," Aubrey said. "What are you doing here?"

"Okay. I live in Seaside. In Seaside I'm seen as the local girl making good. I moved to Seaside right after finishing high school in Portland and I work as a clerk at the toy counter in the old Woolworth's with worn wooden floors, loose candy which is bought by the ounce and scooped into a paper bag. I work six days a week even though I'm continuing school. Sometimes I have to drive to Portland for night courses, so I don't have much time for a social life. My social life is pretty much limited to the local families in Seaside, mostly I know them from meeting them at work.

"I just love my dime store job in Seaside," she explained to Aubrey, "but I have to make more of myself eventually. In Seaside I have a reputation for more than just a clerk. I help the children purchase their prizes at my counter. I know many of the children by name. I know which children are the future engineers from the stories they tell me about their tinker toys and erector sets. I understand the parents' urgency to buy a doll the child will love, even if they can't afford the one that talks and walks. I play toy doctor when children return to the store dragging their doll that has a broken neck or a separated leg or arm. I keep glue, a screwdriver, sewing supplies and paint, all the things a toy doctor needs, under my counter. Sometimes I take the toys home with me to repair, if I don't have time to finish the repairs at work."

"Ceci, how do you manage all that and come here for classes too?"

"I live in a one room apartment on the second floor of the Woolworth building. That saves me money but it's taking me forever to get finished with school this way. It has taken me three years to complete my community college preparation. In another four I should complete my business degree requirements.

"I come into Portland from Seaside several times a week on the train in order to avoid the cost of a motel while I work on a degree in business. Now. Is that enough about me? What about you, Aubrey?"

"I'm a nurse, Cecily. I'm working for the Public Health Department of Portland.

"Cecily, you must stay with me whenever you have to be here in Portland. I have plenty of room. You can have your own closet and a pull-out bed. I promise, no obligations. If you stay with me when you're here you will hear all about me."

"Really?"

"Really. Please do."

"Aubrey, you are a godsend. I won't be much fun though. I'm exhausted most of the time and I don't have money for partying, but we could try it."

So, Cecily moved in with Aubrey during her stints in Portland. She was totally envious of his ability to work, make money, enough to take college courses on a whim. He found her stick-to-ativeness a marvel to behold. Over all their time together she arrived in town just in time to get to school, came home and studied, relaxed a short time with him, briefly joined his friends but immediately headed for home in Seaside where she had to get back to work, when her schooling tasks were complete.

They lived harmoniously together in this manner for two years until Aubrey came home one night and said, "You'll never guess where I'm going."

"Oklahoma?"

"Muang Iai, Thailand. I responded to a request from an American nurse there who needs a break. I should only be gone a month or two, but I might look for a new apartment when I return. Do you want to keep this one in the meantime? It's all paid up for six months."

"Aubrey, you are the most generous person I've ever known, and maybe I'm the most needy you've ever known. Of course, I'd like to keep your apartment but I couldn't pay you back for it," Cecily said.

"Cecily, it's yours. Having you around again has been such a pleasure for me that you've more than repaid me already."

So Aubrey left for Thailand, but the thing is, Aubrey fell in love with Thailand, the people, the culture…the mosquitoes! His one month turned into eight years. At the end of the semester Cecily closed up his apartment, returned the keys to the owner and was on her own again.

Chapter 8

Cecily

2006

When she finally graduated from Lewis and Clark College with a degree in Business Administration, Cecily's neighbors and customers put on a party to celebrate her, right at the lunch counter in Woolworths. She was on her way to obtaining, first her real estate license and then a certification in public accounting. She was also well on her way to living a happy productive life right here in Seaside.

Cecily was immediately hired by LiveRight Real Estate Agency of Seaside. Business was booming and by the end of her first year of employment she won an award as the top salesperson in her agency. Her salary enabled her to put a down payment on a house that she could only have dreamed of. It was right on the ocean front, near town and had a large beach front.

Shortly after Cecily acquired her first home, she was driving home from work on highway 83 one evening when she saw a little black thing on the side of the road. She pulled off and ran back to discover a twenty-pound Doberman puppy. He was whining softly, still alive but unable to stand. He snapped at her helplessly and in pain, while she gently lifted him and placed him on the front seat of her Ram truck and headed back to the veterinarian. She arrived just as he was locking his door.

Now when she reached down to pick up the puppy and carry him into the vet, he licked her all over the face and wagged his rat-like tail.

"You need to put this little guy to sleep," the veterinarian said.

"If it didn't hurt him too much, I'd put him to sleep with my hugs," she said.

"But all four of his legs are broken, probably was run over by a tractor or truck. How will he even stand, let alone be trained to go outside to pee pee and poop? I'm sure he's not trained yet. Too young."

"I'll train him. You just fix his legs and tell me how to manage his pain. The rest is my job," she said. Cecily instead of having him killed, took a week off of work so that she could carry him around until she could get him to walk and squat while still encumbered by four plaster casts. She named him "Romeo-Montague but called him affectionately just Romeo.

When he was able to stumble along on four casts, she took him to the office with her each day. Eventually she took him to doggy physical therapy and after the casts were removed, she spent hours massaging his legs. Romeo seemed to know he had been loved by her and that every minute he enjoyed the sunny beach and warm fireplace was a gift from Cecily.

Chapter 9

Cecily

2013

Then she received that call from the almost forgotten, Aubrey. "I'm coming back to the United States. Can I come and visit you?" Cecily couldn't wait to get to the airport in Portland to pick him up.

"Eight years you've been out of my life, Aubrey, with the Pacific Ocean between us. Here you come back in all your glory and make me feel so special again. When are you going to leave me once more?" Cecily asked as she and Aubrey sat swinging together on her front porch swing. She flipped her blond wedge as she turned to him and stretched her jeans covered legs. First, she reached up with her index finger and gave a cute little twist to his right cheek dimple. Then she gave the swing a push with both feet. She wrapped the plaid blanket more tightly around her shoulders.

It was sunny but fiftyish degrees outside. Soon they would go inside to make Aubrey's first American dinner and relax, together with her dog Romeo, by the fire.

Aubrey, still wearing the khaki shorts that he had worn on the flight back from hot, sunny Thailand, also hugged one blanket around his shoulders and covered his lap with another. He couldn't stop smiling as his whole being felt limber, relaxed, at home. Cecily always said that he smiled more with his dimples than with his mouth and he suddenly became self-conscious of his looks.

"Ceci, I have no idea how long I'll stay with you," he said, using the nickname he had made up for her when we were four years old. "I will leave you if you throw me out. I might leave you if I find a good woman, my dream woman or third, if I find a good job that forces me to move. Otherwise you're stuck with me for a while."

"Maybe it will take another eight years to get reacquainted," Cecily said, hopefully.

"Well, Ceci, my story is like a long travelogue. It's gotta go forward from here. But yours? All the time we had during your college years you never really explained how that all came about. And I resisted prying. I'll resist again if you say so, but I'd really like to know how you got from Broken Bow to Seaside and from a kid to a bustling beautiful entreneur. And, I have to ask, why no significant man or woman in your life?"

"Sometime I'll tell you more. We'll have lots of time to talk," she said. "For now, let's go make dinner."

So, Aubrey settled into his own guest room.

Cecily's home had three bedrooms, one for an office, one that she hoped she would one day need for a guest. Two of the three looked out on the beach. She decorated them in turquoise, pink and shell color to keep the bright beach theme. Her living room had a fireplace, beige, brown and blue tweed overstuffed chairs and sofa, a burgundy and blue round rag rug with a big bed for Romeo right by the fire. The walls were beige and picked up the glow from the fire. The painting over her fireplace mantel was one that Aubrey had painted for her when they were ten years old, of the corn field that could be seen from her home in Broken Bow.

Cecily's kitchen was bright and homey. The eat-in kitchen had a window looking over the beach and wore yellow and white checked gingham curtains.

Throughout the house were her old toys, a doll buggy, a truck, a train engine, toys that were her own, not from the Woolworth toy counter.

Aubrey became good friends with Romeo. He and Cecily eventually shared the details of their personal

76

histories, his grief at the death of his parents, his education, her estrangement from her parents, the birth and loss of her son, Bobby.

Aubrey found his dream job as Director of Memory Care and Rehabilitation Departments at Providence Hospital in Seaside.

Cecily was always there for him but also always encouraged him to develop his own new friends and interests. They were together most evenings for hors d'oeuvres or dinner or an hour by the fire but never demanded the other's attention.

One evening as they sat on the beach side patio with Romeo, enjoying sunset over the Pacific, Cecily said to Aubrey, "It was Romeo who saw me through my most difficult year here. First, I fell in love, then I had to rescue myself from love."

"Why, Ceci? I don't understand, Aubrey said. "Why do you say 'rescue' yourself from the wonderful experience of falling in love?"

"Do you really want to hear it?" Cecily asked. "I've never explained this to anyone else because I don't know if anyone can understand, but I'll try.

"I fell in love with Seamus Geary, your boss at Providence Hospital. I fell really hard."

Cecily saw the surprised expression on Aubrey's face.

"Well I can see how anyone could fall in love with Seamus Geary," Aubrey said. "What in the world happened to you and Seamus? Seems to me like you'd be perfect for each other."

Cecily finally had someone to whom she could tell her story, not exactly 'bare her soul' because even Cecily didn't understand her soul at the time.

Chapter 10

Seamus

2008

Cecily stared at the fire as she began to tell Aubrey about her one-time romance. She was suddenly transported into that other world with Seamus, the world she had hoped to enter, but in the end wouldn't, couldn't open the door, climb the first step.

"When he arrived in 2007, Seamus was hired conditionally by Providence Hospital as an administrative intern. 'I'm an experienced Ophthalmologist,' he told the CEO of Providence. 'I'm not sure I really need an internship or a 'conditionally'. When I worked for Doctors Without Borders in Samoa, I ran the whole operation and did it very well. I have lots of experience. It was only when I ended up in the middle of the war zone in Afghanistan…well that tragic failure had nothing to do with my administration or organizational skills.

'In the ravages of wars in Iraq and Afghanistan I treated much more than eyes and struggled more with staying alive than with organizing. There I found children whose entire face was blown off. They were the lucky ones because they were still alive. Some of them had seen their parents, grandparents and siblings murdered. The last thing some of them ever saw before their eyes were gone, was a screaming dying parent or little sister or brother.' Seamus started to stare into the corner of the room as if he was seeing something other than the CEO who was interviewing him.

Eventually Seamus realized he was unable to face the horrors of war day after day. At first he didn't realize how he had been changed by the experience but when he tried to return to his Ophthalmology practice in the United States each patient who came to see him with a loss of vision, each time he had to break bad news to a patient who would never see well again, he broke down into, sometimes uncontrollable, sobbing.

'Seamus,' the CEO said, 'it took a year for you to realize you were a victim of PTSD and to seek treatment for yourself. Because your whole adulthood has been dedicated to health care, you are hoping to contribute to the health care industry in another way. I want to help you do that not throw you right into another stressful job. Let's take this slowly. I know you can do it and you will in time.'

"And so, when Seamus arrived in Seaside ready to begin his administrative residency, he came to my Real Estate office, LiveRight Inc. searching for a home to purchase here close to Providence. He was forty-six years of age, six feet tall, straight black hair whitening at the edges. He was gentle and pleasant. Although he was dressed casually when I met him, his take on fashion was perfect, navy gabardine shorts, white golf shirt, white socks, navy blue leather shoes, Brooks Brothers head to toe, my type.

"The timing too, was perfect for me. I was finally at a stage in life when I could allow myself the pleasure of a close friend, dating, wasting time. I had an education, a steady job and a home. Seamus fell in love first it seemed to me, not with me, but with that darling four-casted-leg puppy lying beside my desk. Romeo's tail just about beat the varnish off my desk when Seamus got down on his knees to pet him under the ears. Our first date? well maybe you can call it Romeo's date.

'May I see you again, Cecily?' Seamus asked after we had been sitting together viewing available properties on my computer. 'I mean, we don't have to go anyplace,' he said hesitantly. 'I'd just like to come by to see Romeo. I can stop at the cafe` and pick up some coffee and lunch for us. We can just enjoy it here in your office.'

"Well, Seamus," I said, amused at his faltering attempt at getting to know me. "I'm not sure what to make of your offer but of course you can do that. How about a vegetable sub heavy on the green olives."

'Great,' he said, 'What can I bring for Romeo?'

"Oh, Romeo just likes T-bones, thick, medium rare."

"And of course, he called my bluff and brought a big juicy inch thick medium rare T-bone for Romeo. At first our romance, always included our chaperone, Romeo. Seamus was with me when I took Romeo for the x-rays and removal of his casts and came to my home regularly to sit on the beach with me and my dog. About two months later I finally said to him, "Seamus, I think we can leave Romeo home if you would like to go out someplace with just me, like to dinner or a movie."

'Oh sure,' he said. 'I wasn't sure if you'd want that, you know, our age and all.'

"Our age?" I asked. "Why that never occurred to me. Is that a problem for you Seamus?"

'No, of course not, I love younger women,' he was quick to answer.

"And so, we started to date more seriously. We came to know every restaurant, lounge, and theater in Seaside. We checked out the Lighthouse, the Lewis and Clark Salt Works, the aquarium, and Ecola State Park.

"One day in November Seamus came to my house with a surprise. He grabbed me around my waist, swung me around and said, 'Guess what! We have reservations for the weekend at the Gilbert Inn here in Seaside. And Romeo is staying home. Your secretary Sheila has agreed to stay with him.'

"The Gilbert Inn is an up-up-up scale historical hotel here in Seaside. It was there in the Gilbert Dining Room, three months later that Seamus proposed to me. He was so sure of me that he proposed in a full dining room with everyone looking on. When the other diners and the wait staff saw what was happening, this six foot handsome devil down on one knee, and me, a surprised blond woman with a purple flower in my hair, all smiles, waiting anxiously to utter the big 'yes', partners hugged and single people teared as they watched and listened. Of course, I said, 'yes.' How could I not. I loved him so much. And Aubrey, I still do.

"Seamus had just, the previous week, closed on the five-bedroom house he was purchasing. Now we would have two houses. What to do about that? I wondered. Why didn't we foresee our engagement even a week ago? It was time now for us to have some of the serious talks that we had never felt the need for during our squiring days.

'Cecily, how many children would you like to have?' Seamus asked one evening as we sat on my living room sofa in front of the fire.

"I don't plan to have children, Seamus," I replied.

"After a long pause that still makes my hands sweat and my insides tighten up if I let myself feel it, he asked quietly, 'None?'

"None," I said, "You don't have to worry about that, about me getting pregnant. I won't let it happen."

'Worry? I can't imagine a marriage without children. Do you have a medical problem that I don't know about? ' he asked.

"No, I don't have any medical problems," I said. "I just don't want to have children. You don't want kids, at your age, do you Seamus? That's one of the reasons we're so perfect for each other."

"Seamus got up and walked around the room, looked out the window forever, tapped his finger on the windowsill, sat down again a little further from me and turned to study me.

'I'd be willing to adopt children if there is any reason you can't or don't want us to have our own,' he pleaded.

"We were silent for a long time. I studied the confused look in his eyes as he sat there, having wandered around the room without seeing anything except in his puzzled mind.

'Why did you think I would buy a five-bedroom house?' he asked.

"I figured you like a lot of space," I said. "I never thought of discussing children. Because of your age, surely you don't want to start from the beginning raising a family now."

'There you go bringing up my age again…and you say age doesn't matter.

'Cecily, this is the beginning for me, for both of us, whatever our age. I've never had a family and I want one so badly. I gave that blessing up for years because of the importance of the work I was doing. One of the reasons, actually the main reason I came back home from Afghanistan when I did, was so that I would not be too old to be a good Dad, to have a family when I got back. My psychiatrist assured me of what I too believe, that I'm not too old to be a good father."

"Seamus got up from the sofa, grabbed his jacket and headed for the door without his usual kiss, hug, and 'I hate to leave you.' 'Cecily, we both have to think about this now' he said as he walked to the door. 'I've always wanted children. When you and I fell in love I thought, I knew I could dream that it would still be possible in my life.'

"I couldn't speak. How did I miss this essential part of who Seamus was? I was attracted by his gentleness, by his outgoingness. I had seen him having fun with the children we encountered here and there. But I never caught on to their importance for him in his own life. I had assumed too much. I assumed that he was concerned about our eighteen-year age difference because he figured I might consider him too old to start a family. I assumed he wouldn't want to have children at his age. I had thought that that only made him more perfect for me.

"No way did I want to have a child now. That would be too big of an age difference between my son Bobby who would be ten now, and the new child, for the children to enjoy each other. They'd both be like only children. And anyway, I didn't want an obligation to another child in case Bobby ever showed up. And, as for owning a travel agency, I hadn't given up the dream of traveling for my job.

"We stood by the open door, his hand on the door-knob, wanting to get out of my house as fast as he could, but, I think, almost afraid he could never come back. I had the same fear and I couldn't let him go. I started to rattle on endlessly.

"Seamus, I have to let this soak in. I will not deprive you of the possibility of having children. But maybe I'm not the right woman for you to have children with."

'Cecily, I don't want to give you up. It would break my heart to lose you, but I also don't know if I can give up the possibility of having my own family.'

"But, don't you think of you and me as a family? Without children you and I can be more open to other people in our lives. We wouldn't be bound to our children's needs. Our own children wouldn't have to be our priority. We can make the world our family."

Seamus said, 'Teaching a whole new generation how to live good lives, watching my own children grow into giving human beings who can make a difference, that's what children mean to me. And if my own children do not follow that drummer, I will still relish watching them grow into whoever they are, day by day. That is what children mean to me.

'And Cecily, I want the world to have another you when we are gone. The world will be better with a younger you in it.'

"Five minutes ago, my world had been filled with dreams, with a new life trajectory, assurance of a loving partner to fill the black hole I still carried in my heart. In one awkward moment I again began to feel the desolation that had become a part of me.

"When we've both had a chance to think about this some more, we need to talk about it again," I said.

"He pulled the door closed without even a goodbye and was gone.

"As we parted that evening, the plan was to have further discussions about our desire to have or not to have. But both of us knew that there was nothing more to discuss. Life together would mean for one or both of us resentment and tears. I would resent having to put a different child first in my life, ahead of Seamus, ahead of travel, ahead of Bobby. I would have to cozy up to my parents again and give them the satisfaction of seeing me happy with a husband and children, as if they had been right all along.

"Or Seamus would resent my practice of birth control, my superficial happiness with independence from him and our home. One or both of us would carry that little black heart hole during our whole life.

"When I came to return the ring to Seamus, he was only sad, not surprised. He would not take it back. 'It was a gift to the woman I love', he said, 'and my love has not ended, only my plans.'"

Chapter 11

In Truth

2013

After Cecily finished her long story, Aubrey's silent shocked look and head shake told Cecily that he was just speechless. "Are you shocked that I still have dreams of Bobby in my life, that I still feel committed to him?" she asked him.

Aubrey looked at her with his mouth open and tried to form thoughts into words.

"Are you actually making essential life decisions based on the hope of Bobby suddenly showing up, Cecily?" he asked. "He wanted to shake her. He wanted to scream at her. "For God's sake Cecily, let it go. Forgive your parents.

Live your life, you only have one. Enjoy yourself, go forward, not backward any longer!

"Cecily, even if Bobby had lived with you all these years, you would soon be giving him up. Don't you see? We do not own our children. We give them wings, then let them go. We throw them to the wind or to the gentle breeze, whichever they choose, whichever suits them, not us. Then they are gone. Their lives move beyond ours."

Cecily knew then that no one, not even her best friend Aubrey, could understand what her pregnancy had meant to her life. She had never tried to explain her feelings to anyone since that day when she became a sixteen-year-old Mom.

When she took the chance to tell all, to let the beast out of her chest, she watched Aubrey's reaction and suddenly awakened for the first time, to the idea that maybe she had been wrong. Maybe she was wasting, not just her time, but her life. How could she pick it up and go forward after all these years?

Was she getting too old to start again, to change, to be a happier person?   Who was she?

Would Bobby even like her if he found her now?

It was like she was standing in a small hallway, looking at many closed doors afraid to try to open any of them.

It was like she was at the bottom of a long staircase with her life's goal at the top but afraid to climb onto the first step?

"Could Bobby love me now if he found me?" she asked Aubrey.

"Could anyone?"

Cecily had always seemed so in control of everything, so sophisticated so enthused and so at peace. Seeing the depths, the truth of her, what could he possibly say? So, Aubrey, in silence, took her in his arms.

* * * * *

Aubrey remained in Cecily's home for some time at her invitation to him to stay with her. Both Aubrey and Cecily were occupied with their employment but in the evenings found most enjoyment in each other's company. Within six months Aubrey had bought and moved into his own condominium about a mile from the beach where he could view the Pacific Ocean, and Mount Hood, the perfect place for him to enjoy his love for *plein aire* painting. Cecily suggested to Aubrey that he try on-line dating. There he soon found Aida, the woman who was to become the love of his life.

So much pain remained in Cecily's heart while so much joy was reaching Aubrey's. And so much remained unsaid between them. He didn't know what to offer to her. He felt like he was a harvest, a golden wheat field glistening in the breezy sunshine while helplessly watching her wither in a protracted drought. And she could not ask for even a cup of water.

Chapter 12

Two Tsunamis

2016

Cecily and Romeo walked out onto the beach behind her home. What a weird atmosphere this was, kind of a yellowish sky reflected by greenish waves. And hot, a heat wave shouldn't be happening when they were past summer now. Cecily walked close to the water, picking up debris, little junk that seemed to have floated into her usual pristine beach and gotten caught in the sand. An hour ago the tide was coming in as it usually did at this time in the evening. Now when it should be in, it was outbound, about a hundred feet out from its usual position. Romeo was walking around nosing everything that had floated in with unusual excitement. There seemed to be a lot more debris than usual, chunks of wood, even small logs, somebody's slipper, plastic stuff.

Aubrey, who now lived about a mile from the ocean, had invited his new girlfriend Aida, and her newly adopted daughter Jahanara, for the week. Cecily was planning to join them to tour the town. No need to worry, she would join them, give them a nice tour and when they came back, she would check out this tide situation again. There had been an earthquake in Alaska a day or two ago but they hadn't heard of any threats from that all the way down here in Oregon.

After touring Aida, Cecily went back into her own house, took Romeo out for his last leg lift of the evening and came back out to the beach. The tide was in. Normal.

It was the blaring of the emergency siren at midnight that awoke Cecily and made her accept the truth. It was a tsunami warning. The warning system had been installed in the coastal area a few years after the 1964 earthquake in Alaska that caused a tsunami that hit all along the Canadian and northern United States American shorelines.

Cecily grabbed her phone and dialed Aubrey. No signal. Aida and Jahanara were staying at the Gilbert Inn that was near the ocean front just like Cecily's home was. They were in danger and Cecily didn't know if Aubrey had been awakened or if he had already rescued Aida and Jahanara.

Cecily threw on her jeans, grey sweatshirt and flip flops, grabbed her security box of important papers, put the collar and leash on Romeo and headed out the door with him. Thankfully, she had just filled her Ram Truck with gas. It was ready to go.

The street was heavy with traffic making it almost impossible to pull out of her driveway. To complicate the situation the traffic was all going in one direction on both sides of the road. It was headed out and she had to drive opposite the flow of traffic to the Gilbert Inn. The roadway of this tourist town was brimming with pedestrians, bicycles, cabs and buses, and it was pitch dark except for the vehicle's lights. She maneuvered through the traffic gradually but couldn't make any time, couldn't hot rod or hurry, except in her impatient heart. Her anxiety just kept building with no way to get out of her chest. Her insides were experiencing the boiling tea kettle effect with no aluminum cap to whistle and relieve.

Romeo sat there next to her licking her arm. "Stop it," she scolded him, then seeing the hurt look in his eyes she said, "Oh I'm sorry Romeo, you're only trying to help. Just jump in back will you. I have to concentrate." Romeo obediently jumped back and whimpered quietly but continued to lick the back of her neck, probably easing the anxiety that she was passing on to him. When she finally reached the

Gilbert Inn to look for Aida, the Inn was empty. It had already been evacuated. Now what? After all this wasted time driving over here to the Inn, not knowing where its guests had been taken, she had no choice but to head inland toward Aubrey's condo, away from the waterfront without Aida and the child.

In her near panic, she kept her truck window open, waiting for any sound, any clue that would tell her what to do next. Once she got up here away from the waterfront it was eerily quiet so that every dim sound made her jump. There should be noise, panic, dogs barking, people yelling, cars honking. There was nothing but the sound of a pencil rattling in her glove compartment and Romeo shifting his weight back and forth in the back seat. Then came a low rumbling. The noise and quiet was alternating just as the inward/outward bound tide was alternating. Cecily was a mile from the ocean front now, almost to Aubrey's condo when the first wave struck. Suddenly above the silence she heard what sounded like a huge freight train blasting right toward her. On impulse she stopped the truck and squeezed her eyes shut waiting for the crash.

Then the train crashed.

When she opened her eyes, the black wall of water seemed to her like the end of the world approaching, enveloping, and carrying away, everything below her with a roar. The crash of the ocean took away her ability to breathe or to think. In a moment that felt eternal, the first wave was over, carrying with it homes, vehicles, refrigerators and chimneys, wrought iron fences, leaving nothing but moon lit blackness below her. She was not hit by the wave, it hadn't reached this far, but below her, she heard continued heart-beat-like rhythmic rumbling and small cries coming from various distant locations. She could only imagine the next wave or the third one coming yet further and taking her and everything else with it. When she caught her breath, she looked at Romeo and saw the frightened gaze in his silent face.

Then she realized that she was not yet finished fleeing. She had to find Aubrey and the girls Aida and Jahanara. As she drove hysterically toward Aubrey's house she cried out loud to no one present, "Oh Aubrey please be safe, I can't lose you this way." Romeo understood her tears and licked her cheeks from his perch in the back seat. A minute later she was at Aubrey's condo and found Aida and Jahanara huddled behind, on the street side of the building. She honked at them and yelled with hands and mouth, "Where's Aubrey?" He was on the other side of the building checking to see how near to his condo the wave had come. When he saw the truck he ran out to Cecily screaming hysterically,

"Where were you? I could have lost you." He grabbed and hugged Romeo who leaned out the window toward him instead of Cecily for whom his hug was meant.

"Hurry up, get in," Cecily screamed out. "We're out of here. There might be more water. It isn't done til it's done." Aubrey helped Aida and Jahanara up into the truck back seat with Romeo. He ran upstairs into the condo, grabbed a few things like important papers, ran back, hopped in the front seat of the truck and they were gone. They drove seventy miles east, away, and stayed in the first motel they could find that still had room. They spent the whole next day watching the news coverage of the tsunami on the hotel television set. After the second night it looked like the tsunami had settled in place, the town remained flooded, but the violence was gone and residents were returning home.

"I can't go back," Cecily said the second morning.

"I can't wait to go back," Aubrey said. "I know, you've got to be afraid of what you'll find. I think your house made it, Ceci, but we have to go home, we have to know."

"The news reports haven't shown my exact house, but most of the things they've shown on the waterfront are gone."

"It looks like the Gilbert Inn was damaged but is still there," Aida said. "It'll be okay, Cecily. We can help you if it's not. I can find a place to stay for a few weeks so I can help with your house."

"What's wrong with Aunt Ceci"s house?" Jahanara asked.? Romeo wants to go home."

"It might have been damaged by the storm," Aida told her.

"Aunt Ceci, we can build a new one for you. I have a new house where my second mama lives. It's fun to have a new house."

"Everybody can stay at my condo," Aubrey said, "including Romeo. We will make it work. Besides, I will be needed at work now so I have to hurry. back, but if you really don't want to return yet Cecily, you don't need to. I could check out your house for you and then come back and get you."

"No, I really need to face the music," Cecily said. "Jahanara is right. We'll build a new house if we have to. Let's go today."

They drove back to Seaside that morning, heading first for Cecily's house, but were not able to drive all the way to the oceanfront. What was left of the washed-out road was littered with jungle jims refrigerators, upside down vehicles, broken tree trunks. The little bridge over the Necanicum River was too badly damaged to cross. Local people had piled rocks in the river where it was narrowist so that it was possible to walk across them to get nearer to the beach. Cecily begged Aubrey to leave her alone to walk toward her house. She didn't want to drag Aida and Jahanara down there with her to observe her tragedy. But they all insisted on going with her. How could they leave her now?

They parked the truck upside of the washed out bridge and hiked over the rocks and among broken glass, Aubrey carrying Jahanara and Cecily leading Romeo over jagged metal, broken wrought iron fences and through sand and muck to the location about a quarter of a mile distance, where Cecily's house was supposed to be. It was gone. For a minute she wasn't even sure where it had been until she saw her iron fence post. From the post, strangely enough, a piece of the yellow gingham curtain from her kitchen window was innocently waving at them.

Aubrey handed Jahanara to Aida and took Cecily in his arms. After a few seconds she pulled away and looked silently at the ocean then she waded outward and stood in wet shoes with water lapping at her ankles.

Aubrey imagined the collapsed bricks from her fireplace laying there under the sand, but Cecily saw a cold hearth where the extinguished fire had warmed her and Romeo on damp nights. Where Aubrey thought of Cecily's missing or damaged kitchen appliances, Cecily smelled must and mold, the pungent odor that replaced the smell of baking cookies her mother had taught her to bake. While he thought of the cost of replacing the walls and roof of her home, she thought of the walls of the old doll house that her father had made for her and that her mother had given her again at her high school graduation. Her insurance might pay for the diamond ring that Seamus had refused to let her return to him, but it could not pay for her memory of him. Every time she looked at the ring she saw him again, down on one knee before her in the Gilbert Inn restaurant giving her this ring. Aubrey could paint a beach and sunset for her, but he could never replace the painting of her parents' corn field that he had done for her when they were ten, the painting that she had hung over her fireplace.

"Do you want to try to look for some of your buried things now? We will help you find what we can," Aida offered.

"No, not today," Cecily said, but she couldn't turn to leave either. It would feel like tearing the skin from her body. She longed to step out into the water to find her home, to find her life, and bring it back or go down into the sea with it. She continued to stare at the ocean in front of her, not turning to look at Aida and the others. She wanted this to hurt. If it didn't hurt enough, she might forget. What would keep her memories alive when she was absorbed in everyday things, in work, in a sterile new house? Maybe the pain would help her when the years passed, and she wanted to remember.

Suddenly Cecily felt a deep black hole filling her entire being, moving through her from the center of her heart, upward making her feel lightheaded and downward making her legs and arms weak and she groaned and fell on her knees to a squat. It was like another tsunami, her own personal one was hitting. Mostly, it was not the loss of her house or her things that she was feeling. The hole was in the place where her Mom and Dad should be. Suddenly she missed her parents. She wanted to sit down on the sand and cry, cry in her mom's arms. She wanted to hear her dad say, "Everything will be okay." She wanted to be a child again. She stood looking at the ocean that felt as large and wide and as empty as her soul.

* * * * *

Aubrey put his arm around Cecily again and, followed by a silent Romeo and Aida and Jahanara, walked with her back over the rocks and glass to her waiting truck and to his home.

Chapter 13

Cecily

2017

Mrs. Sjordan needed her $2,000.00. Her house was gone, her cat was dead. That one last trip to her hometown, Marstrand, Sweden was now just an impossible dream and Cecily, her travel agent was supposed to get her money back from the Alaskan Ship Line with whom she had booked the trip. "I spent all day trying to get Mrs. Sjordan's $2000 deposit back while I kept hearing from the other end of the phone line, "the rules are…

or

"Did you ever try making peace between an insurance company and a bank both of whom claim to own a house that is gone?" Cecily was helplessly frustrated every day when she returned from work.

"American Airlines agent says my client cannot buy a ticket to return to Jordan because he never came to

Seaside. 'They're idiots. I'm standing here,' he says. 'You can fingerprint me, check my DNA, whatever you want to prove it's me but you can't deny that I'm here. All I want is to go home, to Jordan.'

"The records are gone, Aubrey. People are trying to pretend this never happened and go by their usual systems, process, and rules. It's not working."

"Cecily, maybe you should take a day or two off so you can start looking for a home and office for yourself and Romeo. That might put a little more perspective into your life," Aubrey said naively.

"Are you kidding me? I can't even find a home for anyone else, let alone for me and Romeo. Looking for a home will really put things in perspective, the destroyed home perspective, the desperation perspective." Cecily said painfully. Then she added, "Oh, I'm sorry, Aubrey. I know you must be tired of having the two of us in your little condo. I really do want to move out, I just get overwhelmed by everyone else's problems and find it hard to concentrate on the search for a home for myself."

"Cecily, you know you can stay forever if you want to and I love having Romeo too. He is no problem at all. I just think you will feel better when you can rebuild your own life, own your own castle, maybe buy a new dollhouse or paint some things pink," Aubrey said.

As Cecily had worked at the Woolworth in town all of those years while she was a student, the manager of the Woolworth called her to offer her a space for her business. She was grateful to have a commercial address for her work where clients could find her easily and where she could make use of wifi, electricity and water. But the five and ten did have its drawbacks, in particular, distractions. She found it hard to ignore dime store customers who came by to visit and children who still, after their parents told them about the toy doctor lady, brought toys for her to fix. When she came home in the evening from the makeshift office she had set up in a cordoned off corner of the five and ten, she brought home broken dolls and trucks. In addition, she brought her overload of controversy, anger, and misunderstandings from her broken business.

So, Cecily did take a few days off the next week and found a "perfect" temporary spot for her home and her dog and her business.

"My new 'home' is a warehouse," she said. "It is currently occupied by a displaced family who is awaiting a new home they are having built. I can move my offices into the commercial storefront section immediately. When the family is able to move out of the warehouse, I can occupy the residential section and hopefully, one day I may be able to buy the building. I won't have the beautiful beach front like the one I lost, though. But I don't want a beach front home again anyway, she said not too persuasively. "I loved the one I had, but once was enough. I would be afraid to go to work or to leave Romeo, thinking of all the things that could go wrong."

Aubrey punched the cardboard box of Merlot that was sitting on his kitchen island and pulled out the plastic spigot from the box. He was trying to buy time to figure how to approach this new subject. He pulled out two wine glasses and filled them without asking if she wanted a drink. When he handed a glassful to her she reached for it without question.

"Hey Ceci, tell me about Oscar's friend. You know, the Indian guy, the one from our town, the one you said you knew so well as a kid. You said you were with him a lot the week you spent in Broken Bow when you went to the Memorial for my parents."

"Oh, Rainbird?" she asked, her blue eyes breaking into an immediate sparkle when she repeated his name.

"Yeah, him, what's he like now, all grown up?" Aubrey asked.

"Well, he's pretty hard to describe." She thought about it. "You know those round -bottomed clowns that you push to one side and they roll back to the other? Well Rainbird is like one of those. You push him to his sad side and he rolls back to his funny side. Or you push him to the sunny side, and he rolls back to being serious and kind and sometimes sad."

"Wow!" Aubrey said.

"Yeah. His eyes are dark and quick and slightly hooded. And oh, those cheek bones. He's a big guy, but all muscle. Big shoulders to carry the weight of the world but not an ounce too much fat. He's got this big heavy dark brown, neatly trimmed beard and a moustache that turns up on the corners like the barbershop quartet man in a straw hat. He's got straight short dark hair. He's gruff and soft all in one. His first name is Nicco. Nicco Rainbird, but Rainbird fits him so well that everybody uses that for his handle."

"Cecily, you sound very interested in him," Aubrey said.

"Me? No," she said. "But I do like him a lot. He lives in overalls with a bib and boots and smokes a corn cob pipe. Not my type, but I do enjoy him."

"What kind of work does he do?" Aubrey didn't need to ask; he could have guessed.

"He rescues broken down animals, horses, mules, he has a barn owl with one wing and a dog with two legs that runs around with his hind end on a little cart with a poop hole in it. Niko spends his time taking care of the animals, returning wild ones to nature when possible, collecting donations to help the animals in return for doing little jobs for people, you know, handy-man stuff. He has goats who mow his lawn, a blind Australian shepherd who herds his few sheep, he gives all the animals jobs. He sits on his back porch sharing peanuts from the shell with his two-legged and blind dogs. Says he accumulates the shells for bedding for the small animals.

"You know an awful lot about him for someone who only spent a few days with him in town," Aubrey commented.

"Well, we've been writing, emailing and texting," Cecily said. "He makes me feel alive. Like yesterday he told me about a deer that got caught in a fence. The wild life people were called and were able to get it loose but it didn't run away when it was freed so they called Rainbird to pick it up and nurse it back to health before they could release it. He found shreds of the barbed wire jammed into its hooves. When he got them all out the deer ran free.

"Weird thing is you'd never expect a guy like Rainbird to be an intellectual, but he is. He's read "War and Peace." He subscribes to Environmental Science and Astronomy Journals. Doesn't know much about politics but knows everything about science. His favorite free-time place is the library."

"Cecily, it sounds like this guy is an exciting friend for you."

"Well, he's interesting, but he's not my type," she insisted. "I mean, I'm a businesswoman. I've graduated from college and have master's degrees. I'm a licensed real estate agent and a CPA, and I'm good at all that. No, I belong here. And Rainbird certainly belongs there in Oklahoma."

"And are you happy here with your degrees and licenses and your work in Seaside…and with your distant relationship with your mom and dad?" Aubrey asked her; just had to get that last phrase in.

No answer from Cecily.

"Cecily, do your parents like Rainbird?" he asked her.

"I don't know, I haven't asked them. I'm sure they know him because Oscar brings him around. In fact, Rainbird told me that he painted my parents' house for them. Guess they must like him all right."

Then, after another long pause Cecily said,

"Now don't you go putting doubts in my mind just because I lost my house and all." After some thought she added, "I guess my parents know what it is like to lose a child now that they've lost me for so many years."

Aubrey wondered if she ever thought about..." Cecily, what do you know about that little grave on your parents' property? Did you once tell me that it was the grave of your brother? How did your parents lose him? Do you remember him?"

Cecily looked at Aubrey with a startled look in her eyes. Her whole face froze with a dumbfounded expression. Her eyes spasmed east and west. Her silence felt intense. Her 'aha' moment. She suddenly connected her loss of her son with her parents' loss of their son. All these years she had been punishing them, not realizing nor remembering that they knew exactly what it felt like to lose a son. At least her son was still alive hopefully, having a good life. Their son was gone, forever gone. Cecily alone was left to be their comfort.

How did she miss being aware of their story all these years? Cecily jumped up bumping into and knocking over her glass of wine. The glass broke but she didn't notice it. She made a bee line for her room and Aubrey could hear her sobbing through the door.

Cecily wanted so badly to call her parents, just hear their voices and say, "How did you do it? Why didn't you re-mind me?" She wanted to put together the pieces of who they were and who she was, but she was exhausted and didn't have the nerve to call them immediately. She had to deal with herself first. Her despairing cry kept up for a long time gradually diminishing until she apparently fell asleep.

Chapter 14

Cecily

2017

The next day Cecily moved her office into her warehouse and was quiet when she came home in the evening. Aubrey didn't know if it was right to bring up that conversation about her parents again, so he was waiting for her to be the one to initiate the conversation. Then one evening she came back to his place after working all day, stepped heavily into the house, as if in a daze, even forgot to close the door behind herself. Romeo was still staying with Aubrey when she was at work all day. When she came in he jumped up and down in front of her as he always did. She usually responded to him with a hug and a twinkle in her eyes but this time she said, "no Romeo," and headed straight for her room instead of even saying hello to Aubrey.

After fifteen minutes she returned to the living room and explained, "My mom phoned and said she had a call yesterday from a twenty-year-old man named Robert Ainsley who is searching for his biological parents. He has followed the trail so far to the last name James and then to my parents."

"Oh my god, Cecily! It's Bobby! Why aren't you excited? Did you call him? Is it him?" Aubrey couldn't contain himself with happiness for her but she actually she was glum, maybe frightened, spoke few words, had a straight face, like trying to keep control of her emotions. Was she afraid to know the truth about him, now that finding him was possible, was real?

"No, Aubrey, I haven't called him. I don't know what to say. I just don't want to get my hopes up. What if it's not him?

"My mom told him that she has a daughter in Seaside who is single and has no children. She told him that she would discuss this call with her daughter, and he should call back in a week.

"What if it is him and I've lost him again?"

"...and it's your mom's fault?" Aubrey asked.

"Cecily, he has found you," Aubrey said. "But you have to take a chance. You won't want to live with yourself if you don't. Call your mom and tell her you want to talk to him. You can't expect your mom to know what to do because you've been so distant from her. Your mother loves you Cecily. She will do anything she can to help."

"But can Bobby ever forgive me for giving him away?" she whimpered and almost whispered, "and can my parents forgive me for how badly I've hurt them?"

"I think that Bobby will probably be very grateful to you for giving him life and a chance for a good childhood," Aubrey said hopefully. But your parents Cecily, I have to ask you the hardest question. Have you forgiven your parents?"

Cecily's eyes held so much pain Aubrey could barely stand to look at her, but he did, and he waited.

"I didn't understand them. As a teenager I thought they didn't know anything. I thought that they didn't understand my pain in losing my son. I thought that they didn't want to understand that I was grown up enough to make my own decision. I forgot until now that they also lost their son. They did know. Maybe the way I carried on brought all of their pain in losing their son, back to them again. That's what they would have to forgive me for. It's too much."

"Maybe."

"But what can I do now? It's been twenty years. I'm almost thirty-five years old. I've been an adult for a long time. I should have forgiven them a long time ago."

"Can you forgive yourself, Cecily, for all those years, for all those choices?"

He waited.

"Cecily, now is all that counts. You acted out what was in your heart when you were sixteen. You will act out what is in your heart now. Your parents will know."

Cecily went alone for a walk-through town, down toward the beach, past new store fronts where she looked at new clothes and new hairdos but didn't see them. Then she came home and tried to watch television but kept getting up and walking around the room. Then she went to her room and changed to her p.j.s. When she came back to the living room where Aubrey was sitting, she said,
"I called my mom. She gave me Bobby's phone number. My mom said that if it is him, we can arrange to meet at the Oklahoma farm if I want to. I could hear my dad in the background saying, 'tell her this, tell her that, ask her...' Then my mom said I should please hurry and to let them know what happens just as soon as I can."

"Cecily, they are so excited to meet him. He is their only grandson you know. And they will be especially excited to have you back in their lives."

"But things have been ice cold between me and them for so long. I've hurt them too much to ask them to help me now."

"Cecily, take one step at a time. If this is your Bobby, you must work things out with your parents for his sake. If it's not your Bobby, you must work things out anyway for your sake and theirs. They are getting old without you. Don't wait too long. This is your big chance. You can do it."

Chapter 15

Home

2017

"Aubrey, I'm afraid." Cecily gripped the arms of her chair as if she was seeing a live ghost, trying desperately to back away from it. "I've been so wrong about my parents. I just didn't understand them, and they didn't know how to explain themselves to me. I didn't really give them the chance to try."

"Call them," Aubrey said.

Cecily got up from her chair and went for another walk. She hiked like a Chinese soldier, as if she was going toward someplace, she had to be, someplace where her problem would be solved. The ocean was a mile away from Aubrey's place but it was still the ocean that drew her true emotions from her. It felt like the waves that washed her feet and splashed her face with coolness also took her heat and pain back out to sea with the water. The vastness, the foreverness of the sea, held a part of her home and a part of her heart and called her to things bigger than the moment.

She sat down on the sand facing the sea and allowed its coolness to lap over her feet and the bottom of her jeans.

She dug her phone from her back pocket and dialed.

"Your parents told me," Nicco said, when he answered on the first ring. "They said that all the facts check out. It sounds like your son has found you."

"Yes," she said matter of factly. "Bob Ainsley was born May 21st, 1997 in Portland, Oregon and adopted May 22nd by Robert and Rebecca Ainsley of Eugene, Oregon. Now he is studying at the Art Institute in Chicago."

"Rainbird, do you think I could come home to my parents?"

* * * * *

When Cecily arrived back at Aubrey's place two hours later, she continued to seem pensive and uncertain. Aubrey asked, "Did you call your parents?"

"I called Rainbird," she said.

"Why Rainbird?" he asked.

She didn't answer the question.

"He said my parents asked him to help move their furniture around. They're changing their office space back into a bedroom and cleaning the house. He said my dad was out by the sheep this morning when he arrived and was singing 'Oh What a Beautiful Morning.' Sounded like croaking, like a cow's version of the song," he said with a hee haw. Rainbird says he hasn't heard him singing loud like that for a long time."

"Cecily, call them," Aubrey said, finally getting impatient with her.

Cecily went out onto Aubrey's balcony, closed the sliding glass door, and sat down. Aubrey watched her pick up her phone and start to dial, then she hit the off button and laid the phone down. Then she picked it up and dialed again, then hit off, and laid it down a second time. Finally, she dialed a third time and held it to her ear. She conversed this time for about ten minutes. Then she got up and came back in.

"I'm going to Broken Bow for Thanksgiving," she said with a wavering voice. "I'm driving the truck so Romeo can go with me. My Mom said he's welcome and that he can be an inside dog while we're there since that's what he's used to. She wants me to come a week before Thanksgiving because she's going to invite Bobby for Thanksgiving. That way she can help me get reacquainted with the town before Bobby comes so I can show him around. She says that not much has changed there since I lived there twenty years ago except now there are vacation homes and always tourists. She says most of the tourists stay in airbnb places now so there aren't really any more motels or hotels than there used to be, just the old ones. But I should come early anyway to have a look-see."

"And what if Bobby doesn't want to come there for Thanksgiving?" Aubrey asked her.

"Oh, he will," she answered.

"Cecily, be prepared. If he doesn't want to or can't come at that time, are you prepared to disappoint your parents again? Or, will you go anyway and give them that happiness?"

"What should I do Aubrey?"

"You know what you should do, Cecily," he said.

Bobby agreed to come to the James's farm for Thanksgiving as long as his parents, Robert and Rebecca Ainsley and sister Julie were also invited. Evelyn and Wally would have built an addition on the house and hired servants if necessary, to have the Ainsley's there for Thanksgiving, and of course, to have Cecily.

By the first of November Cecily couldn't stand the wait any longer. "I'm leaving tomorrow," she said. "My employees are ready for me to be gone. My bags are packed. And look at Romeo. He's pacing around behind me on sentry duty. He knows something's up. Nicco says my parents can't wait for me to be there. I might as well go."

* * * * *

Cecily called her parents when she was an hour out of Broken Bow. She called Rainbird too, but he said he would not be coming over until the next day because he wanted to be sure "mama and papa bear had time with baby bear first."

When Cecily pulled up in front of their house the two of them were waiting out in front, had been waiting out front of the house for the whole hour since she called. She could tell that they were nervous too, as she was, by the way her dad beckoned her mom forward as he stood back and by the way her mom moved from one foot to the other. One of her mom's feet was charging ahead, could not be stopped, the other held her back, unsure. So Cecily reached wide open with her arms to both her parents and they both grabbed her together into a hug that felt warm and belonging. None of them could breathe. It was like they were all finally home.

Cecily started to say, "Mom and Dad, I'm so sorry..."

"Now hush," Dad said.

"Are you hungry? Mom asked, like that was all that mattered.

"I love you both so much," Cecily said, and it was all over. The past was past in a flash. The now was forever now. The tension in Cecily's shoulders eased.

"Don't forget the dog," Dad said. "Bring him in the house now. We have your bedroom all fixed up with a nice big dog bed for Romeo. I hope he likes it."

Cecily got Romeo out of the truck who did his stretch-like bow to Wally and then to Evelyn, then after quickly watering a rose bush, followed the trio into the house.

Cecily had been trying for a month, to work out the conversation they would have about being sorry and forgiveness and how they would move forward. As it turned out no conversation wasn't needed at all. She and her parents were able to look at each other, couldn't stop smiling at each other. They were content to share lunch, though their real hunger was already assuaged before they sat down to lunch. Probably the most important thing said between them was Dad's "Now hush".

After they had lunch together filled with excited conversation about the drive here, Romeo's perfect dog behavior in the truck and the preparation of this house for Cecily and the Ainsley's, Mom said, "now let me show you your room." Cecily's room was an adult version of her teen-age room. Gone were the posters of Billie Joe Armstrong and Green Day Rock replaced with a painting of Seaside ocean front. Gone were the clutter of boots, thongs, saddle shoes and patent heels that always lay beneath an empty shoe rack, replaced with a white shabby-chic dresser. The room was freshly painted the same cloud blue it had been and the full-size bed with multi-colored quilt was the one she remembered. The big grey cushion beside the bed was for Romeo. He knew immediately that it was his and jumped on it to claim it making Wally throw his head back and laugh hilariously.

"Let me show you where Bobby will sleep," Evelyn said and led them all up the stairs to the attic room that had been re-done for him. It had rustic medium colored wooden panel walls, maple wood flooring and blue gingham curtains over the french windows that looked out over the sheep pens.

"I hope Bobby will love being here," Cecily said. She had visited his parents and little sister Julie in Eugene, Oregon, in preparation for her meeting with Bobby here. She knew what a good life Bobby had had growing up. That allayed her concerns that he might resent the loss of this beautiful home. He had been loved. She knew that he was now, living out his dream at the Art Institute in Chicago.

"I must call Rainbird and let him know I arrived safely," Cecily said. Wally and Evelyn gave each other the knowing eye. They were happy for the connection between Nicco Rainbird and Cecily, whatever it might mean in the future.

"And I have to call Aubrey's folks, his uncle Oscar and Aunt Charlotte," Evelyn said. I promised to let them know right away when you arrived safely."

Chapter 16

Nicco Rainbird

2017

Cecily's dad called from outside her bedroom door at seven a.m. "Rainbird is on the phone for you. Should I tell him to call back later?"

"I'll be right out," Cecily said.

Dad smiled. He knew she wouldn't miss Rainbird's call, even if she was not used to such an early start. Cecily burst out of her door pulling a robe on as she walked and was followed by Romeo bumping into her heels. "Hey Cecily, how about a ride with me over to see Oscar and Charlotte and say hello," Rainbird said. "I'll pick you up in an hour if you want to go."

"Of course, I want to go," Cecily said. She was dressed in ten minutes and when she got to the kitchen, Evelyn had bacon frying in a pan and eggs basting in the grease.

"Mom, you'll have me fat before I go home," Cecily said, but she ate greedily sitting at the family kitchen table with Mom offering her more coffee, more toast, more bacon, to keep a conversation going.

Cecily was glad to hear Rainbird's horn honk. "Gotta go Mom, thanks for breakfast," she said, kissed her quickly on the cheek and was gone.

Although her first day with her parents portended nothing but good to come, being hopeful and cautious all the time, in all of their conversation, was stressful for her. Romeo had followed her out and knew to jump up to the bed of the truck. He lay down in the back of the pickup on a load of straw that Nicco used to carry animals that needed cushioning when riding.

"How did it go yesterday with your parents?" Rainbird asked when she hopped in his old black Chevy pickup truck. Cecily was happy for the chance to be alone with Rainbird.

She took a deep breath and let it out with a sigh. "Good," she said, "only maybe too good. All three of us are trying so hard to avoid hurting each other. We still haven't had any serious talk about what happened twenty years ago or during the twenty years since. I started to say I'm sorry for all my distance and that I hoped they could forgive me, but my dad stopped me and said, 'Now hush.'"

"What then?' Nicco asked.

"Then my mom said lunch was ready. Then they showed me around the house, my room, all beautifully re-done, Bobby's room in the attic, his parents' and sister's room that used to be the office." Then my dad and I went out to the paddock to see the six sheep that Dad is still caring for. Then we all took a nap and I unpacked.

"Then we had dinner and talked about my visit to Bobby's parents. I told them about the Ainsley home in town with two lots of land, all mowed. I told them how his parents showed me pictures from his birth to now, Bobby's baby butt, Bobby in the bathtub, Bobby getting on the school bus, Bobby graduating. And lots of pictures of Bobby with his little sister Julie. He has a little sister who was born naturally when he was four and has a mild case of cerebral palsy.

It seemed like they wanted me to see his whole child-hood in one sitting. I told my parents it was hard for me to see what I missed but…It's funny. It's hard to admit even to myself. I was almost glad that I didn't have to go through that whole childhood with him in real time, spread out over eight-een years. I didn't have to see him throwing up or having croup and fevers and falling off his front porch. I didn't have to sit through graduation from day care, graduation from kindergarten, graduations from eighth grade and high school like they did in the eighteen-year version of his life. I was actually glad when showtime was over and I could go to bed and be alone. It felt like Bobby was a stranger and it was spooky to see him looking just like my dad.

"He does look like you, Dad, I had told my father. His pictures as a teen looks just like my dad did in the pictures I've seen of him at that age."

"Then my parents asked me lots of questions about Julie, his little sister and I told them that Bobby seems to have been very protective of her and loved her very much. Both my parents said they were happy that he seems to have had a good childhood. I'm a little upset that we still haven't had any discussion of my leaving them or their tricking me or forgiveness on either of our part."

Cecily and Rainbird were silent for a long while. Cecily could see the brain waves in Rainbird's head mulling over her comments. "Well what do you think I should do to get them to talk about it?" she finally asked him.

Rainbird pulled the truck over to the side of the road and stopped the engine so he could concentrate on this important conversation. He turned in his driver's seat and bent his right knee up onto the bench seat so he could look more directly at Cecily. "Dear Cecily," he said, looking straight into her eyes. "What do you think 'Now hush' means to your dad?"

"I suppose it means that he doesn't want to talk about it," she said.

"No Cecily, 'now hush' means so much more than that. 'Now hush' means, not just that you are forgiven, but that there is nothing to forgive. It means your dad knows that just as he and your mother did, you too always did the best you could. It means that you were never absent from their lives even though they weren't seeing you. You were always right here with them in their hearts. It means that they know, even if you didn't, that they were always in your goals, thoughts, in your heart too.

"Cecily, you were for them like a star on a cloudy night. Even though the stars can't be seen when it is cloudy, they are still there, and they are still shining. 'Now hush,' means that your parents knew your love for them when they could not see or hear you. They were like people who are deaf and cannot hear but they know, or like blind people who cannot see, yet still perceive."

Cecily now realized the poignance of her parents' response to her. It was not avoidance. They had dived into the depths of the ocean and had been there so long, that now they wanted to feel the air in their lungs as they broke above the surface of the sea. They did not want to talk about their fear or sadness. The time would come, but not now. Their silence about her absence meant they were at peace with her return.

"Cecily, when you rescued Romeo, I'm sure he snapped at you in his pain, and fear. Do you think he hated you? Of course not.

"Do you think you were abandoned by your parents during this time? Your parents are doing a welcoming, happy dance of forgiveness. Don't ruin it. They do not need your repentance.

"Now you need to follow their lead and leave all your coldness behind. Now you need to be their loving, warm, funny daughter. Learn all you can about them and open to them all of your experiences. Be vulnerable. Let them lead. Share your life story with them one experience at a time."

"Cecily, people of their generation don't talk about everything, but they do understand everything."

"Oh Rainbird, I've been so wrong about them.

"One day I was with Aubrey and he asked me about my brother who died. That's when I suddenly realized what my parents have suffered. They knew very well what it was like to lose a child and they never burdened me with their pain. They shouldn't have had to lose me too."

"You were a child Cecily. Remember when you meet Bobby, that he was also a child and did not experience the sense of loss that you did when he was growing up. It was only when he was older that he felt the need for you, to make his own story complete, to understand where he came from and why he lost you. It was then that he began to hope that you would feel the same way and welcome him. You are now about to do that and it's exactly the same thing that your parents are doing for you."

"It's too much, Rainbird. I can't stand all this emotion and wondering," she said.

"You can and you will, Cecily." Rainbird reached over and took her in his arms and kissed the top of her head. She felt his small soft beard on her forehead. He smelled of hay. The bib of his overalls was still damp from the milk he had been feeding the orphaned baby lamb before he picked Cecily up. His plaid cotton flannel shirt felt warm, made her feel like it could put her to sleep.

Finally, Romeo let them know it was time to move along when he scratched the rear window of the truck. Charlotte and Oscar would be waiting for them. This momentous part of their lives was waiting for them, Romeo was right, it was time to move along. Rainbird turned and put the truck in gear and jerked to a start while Cecily scooted over into the center of the bench seat to sit nearer to Rainbird.

* * * * *

"Tomorrow I want to take you shopping," Evelyn said to Cecily. I want to buy something just for you, something you will keep to remember this special trip, by."

"Mom, do you think I'll ever forget one moment of this trip?"

But you're on. I'd love to have that special gift from you," Cecily replied.

"So, think of anything else you'd like to buy or do while we're out. Dad will mind Romeo. We can have lunch at Steven's Gap or Grateful Dead or Huckleberry's or, oh you choose the place. Maybe you can help me buy a Grandma's first present for Bobby while we're there. I have no idea what he would like."

And so the next morning at 10:00 the minute the stores would be open Evelyn and Cecily headed for downtown Broken Bow in Cecily's truck. "I want to drive so that I start to learn my way around again," Cecily said.

After they parked, they headed down Main Street and Evelyn pulled Cecily into the first Jewelry shop. Cecily chose a thin silver chain with a silver half-of-a-heart on it and bought the same for her mom. "We are both only half of a heart without the other," she said to Evelyn. "I wish I had known that sooner."

Cecily kept recalling her morning conversation with Rainbird. "Be vulnerable, be an open book for your parents now." And so she would try. She was going to find that much harder than just saying 'I'm sorry.' So at lunch at the Blue Rooster Cecily told Evelyn about her experience of seeing the empty beach site, her lost home after the tsunami. "I couldn't even think when I watched the waves washing up where my home used to be. But I could feel. What I felt most was emptiness, not just my lost house on the beach, but my lost home in Oklahoma, my lost parents, and I needed you then."

"Cecily, you should have called or come home then."

"I know Mom, so many 'should haves' in my life."

"But look what we have now, Cecily," Evelyn said. "You know, one never knows what it feels like to be pain free until having had pain, it goes away.

"How about some bread pudding. It's the best in Oklahoma, warmed with pumpkin sauce."

"Mom, what can I buy for Dad?" Cecily asked as they were rounding up their shopping trip.

"Nothing, dear," Evelyn replied. "I've tried over and over to buy things for him. He really doesn't want anything. I always find my gifts later still in the box they came in.

"Mom, wait out here just a few minutes. I just had an idea of something I can get for him. I'll be right back." Cecily ducked into a gift store. She provided the clerk with a picture she had taken of Wally with Romeo. They would transfer the picture to canvas material and make it into a pillow. She could pick up the pillow before Thanksgiving.

They had decided to bring Bobby shopping and let him pick out his own gifts, but Evelyn bought for him a small teak artist-carved box in which to place her note telling him of the planned shopping trip and the gifts he could choose.

And so passed the two weeks awaiting Bobby's arrival. Cecily spent most of the time out on the ranch with Dad and was often joined by Rainbird.

"Come on inside and have a beer," Evelyn called to Rainbird one day.

"Can't I'm too dirty to sit on your beautiful furniture," he responded. Then Wally hollered, "Rainbird, come here, I need you."

Rainbird opened the door and dashed in. "What do you need, Wally?"

"I need you to sit down here and tell us about what happened today. And I need a little dirt on this furniture to help me feel at home in my own house," Wally said. "Now here's a Hamms Beer for you. Just sit and talk."

Rainbird sat as ordered. "Okay. Let me think what you want to hear. You know Wally, It just ain't in my nature to put any critter down as they say, or kill em as I say. But this morning I had to do it. That hawk I took in last week with the missing claws, it was buzzing every other bird and animal it could, flew right into the eye of my goat. It isn't in the nature of a hawk to act like that but it attacked everybody it could, day and night. It wasn't any use to keep it all alone in a cage forever so I finally put it to sleep so it wouldn't feel anything and then, kaboom."

"What do you do when you 'kaboom'? Wally asked.

"As long as it's really asleep I can just chop its head off," said Rainbird. "It won't feel a thing. But I hate taking a life. But then, I'd hate thinking of it out in nature helpless when a coyote comes along."

"Rainbird, you did the best thing, I'm sure. Now can you tell me a good story from today? Don't leave me with a downer like that," Evelyn interjected.

"Sure, there's always one good thing a day. Like that squirrel run right up my leg to the pouch in my bib to get a pecan. I named her 'Bantam' cause she's like one of them aggressive hens. Now that she got a pecan, she'll be back every day, you'll see.

From then on, a short visit from Rainbird was expected every afternoon. His stories and just his presence helped speed up the time as they all awaited anxiously for Bobby's arrival the Monday before Thanksgiving.

Chapter 17

Bobby

2017

Romeo paced back and forth in front of the white frame country home following a few feet behind Cecily, watching her determined walk.

Cecily's parents watched her intensity too, both of them praying silently that her meeting would go well, that she would find the peace that had eluded her since her teen years. Wally fidgeted with Evelyn's blouse collar, pulling it up over her jacket collar. Evelyn forced a smile at him, then shrugged her shoulders, pulling away from him. "Is his room clean?" she asked Wally.

"You've been upstairs three times this morning to check on it. You know it is clean," Wally said impatiently

Then, right on time, the dust rose out there where their pebble drive meets the highway. All four of them tensed in place as they listened to the tires crunch the pebbles and saw the yellow Camaro convertible pull thoughtlessly, confidently up in front of their house.

A six-foot-tall auburn curly haired young man jumped out. He was wearing a navy double-breasted sport coat with gold buttons and tan slacks. He approached Wally directly and held out his hand to shake Wally's. He looked for all the world like a businessman coming to close a deal on buying the house.

"Hi, I'm Bob," he said to Wally. "Are you Mr. James?"

Wally smiled uneasily, not wanting to be the focus of this exchange. Cecily stopped dead in her tracks and watched, trying to silence the growling of her nervous stomach, and Romeo stopped at her side, looking up at her questioningly.

"Bob, this is Evelyn, your grandmother," Wally said as he motioned his wife forward. Bob reached his hand out to Evelyn to shake her hand just as he had shaken Wally's.

Cecily forced her foot to take its first step forward, then her second step. Although she had seen the young man's pictures, she didn't realize that when she saw him she would suddenly realize that she was looking at a younger image of her dad, a male image of herself.

"You must be my mom," Bob said to her as she approached him. She nodded. "And this is Romeo your brother," Cecily said, trying to add humor to this intense moment.

Bob reached out his hand to shake hers, then bent down and gave a big hug to the dog who backed away from him warily.

Wally, always willing and able to save the day, said, "Welcome to our home Bobby."

Then Evelyn gathered her courage and said to him, "You must be hungry Bobby. Come in and see the house. I have some lunch prepared."

"You can bring your things in with you. I'll show you your room," Wally said.

As Bob unlocked the trunk of the Camaro, Cecily called on all her resources and, like an army general leading his men into battle, she told her emotions to 'charge!' "Bobby, just hold still a moment and let me look at you," she said. "I've been waiting for this moment for twenty years." She reached out with both hands and grabbed his upper arms as he straightened up, looked down at her then broke into a big and genuine smile. He had straight white teeth and

140

a dimple on one side of his mouth. Cecily noticed that he was perspiring even though it was cold out. She felt relieved to realize that he had been nervous too only had a little too much bravado to let on that he was nervous about this meeting.

"You look like my dad," Cecily said.

"Do you think so?" he asked.

"Exactly. You can look at him and see your future," she said.

Cecily pulled Bobby forward and kissed him on the right cheek bone. "We can talk later," she said. "For now, get your things and come on in."

He grabbed a duffle bag, slammed closed the trunk and winked at Romeo who was obviously on sentry duty not intending to let this stranger out of his sight.

Wally led Bob up to the attic bedroom which he had worked so hard to prepare perfectly but Bob immediately crashed his head into the slanted ceiling of the room. "Sorry, I'm a klutz," he said.

"No, you're not a klutz, you're tall, Bob. Why don't you just put your things there and Let's have lunch. You can come back afterwards to settle in and make yourself at home up here."

Lunch was eaten too quickly, everyone uncomfortable with each other as evidenced by their discussion of the weather. They also talked about Bob's drive here from Chicago but unfortunately, it was a smooth ride, so it didn't provide for much conversation. Cecily told Bob about how much she had enjoyed meeting his parents and sister and seeing his baby pictures.

"My mom probably showed you how cute my bottom was and all my scabbed knees," he blushed. "She shows those to everybody. It's so embarrassing."

Bob was relieved when Wally offered him a tour of the sheep pens and and paddock and all the property where the sheep were grazing. He could be more comfortable outdoors with Wally. Didn't feel like he had to meet expectations with him like he did with the women.

"Can I ride on your tractor?" Bob asked when they were out behind the house. "I've never ridden on a tractor before. Wait, I better grab my jeans before we go out there. I'll be right back out."

They bounced along, Bob egging Wally on to drive at roller coaster speed. This was entertainment, not a work vehicle for him. Then, through exhilarated laughing he yelled, "Hey Wally, stop here for a minute, will you?" He jumped down from the tractor and pulled up purple, white, yellow wildflowers. "My first bouquet for my grandmother," he said.

He proudly presented the flowers to Evelyn when they got back to the house. She reached up, pulled him down by the neck, kissed him on the cheek and said, "Memories of my young Wally." Evelyn found a small metal sprinkling can and filled it with water to hold the flowers. Then she removed one flower of each color to place in a glass of water by her kitchen sink. Then she took Bobby by the hand and led him into the room that would be for his parents. She placed the sprinkling can holding the flowers on the bedside cabinet between the beds. These will be a beautiful welcome for your mom when she arrives tomorrow," she said.

After some time in his attic room, trying to gather courage to join Cecily, Bobby left the house to walk around the grounds alone. Cecily too, was looking for courage when she paced around, then back to the kitchen where Evelyn, in cotton house dress, hair in a bun, hands covered with flour was kneading dough for pumpkin bread.

"Can I help?" Cecily asked thinking, *'please say yes, I need something to do.'*

"You know, honey, I've been thinking," Evelyn said. "Bobby's parents will be arriving in the morning. It might be a good idea for you to have some private time together with him before then."

"I would love to do that, but I don't know how to approach him," Cecily hesitated.

"He seems like an open and caring young man, Cecily. And after all, it was Bobby that started the ball rolling that led to his eventually finding you. I bet he'd love the opportunity to talk with you alone. He probably has all kinds of questions, if you give him a chance.

"He just went out for a walk by himself. You could find him out in the gardens. Maybe all you'll have to do is listen," Evelyn said. She took Cecily by the arms getting flour all over her arms and blouse. "Cecily, You will know what to say."

Cecily didn't even notice the flour. "Okay Mom, I'll do it. Here I go," Cecily said as she worked up the courage.

Cecily walked around the property looking for Bobby until she finally saw him ambling along the side of the road away from the house. As she approached, she saw he carried a wheat-shaped piece of grass. He put it to his mouth to suck on, like he was trying to get the feel of being a country boy. Cecily came near and said quietly, "Bobby?"

"Oh, Hi," he said to her seeming a little uneasy.

"I thought it might be a good time for us to talk, to get to know each other better," she said.

"Okay," he said.

"You must have some questions for me," Cecily said.

"I have a million, but I don't know where to start," Bobby said.

"How about, 'who is my dad?' or 'why did you give me up?' or, you can tell me if you're angry at me," she said.

"I think I'm too bewildered to be angry," he said. "Looking at this farm and meeting you and your parents makes me imagine what my life would be like if I had been raised by you. It seems like it would have been a wonderful life. I'm trying to imagine why. Why couldn't you have kept me?

"And yet, I love my parents and Julie. I wouldn't give them up for anything, And my whole life is so different than it would have been, my art career, my opportunities, my friends. So, am I angry? No. But confused. Way!

"I dreamt of many versions over the years, of what you must be like, of why you gave me up, but you're none of those."

"What did you imagine, Bobby?"

"Well you could have been married to someone else besides my Dad and had to keep the baby a secret. Or you could have been a prostitute. Or you could have been a cold businesswoman who preferred climbing the ladder at work to having a kid in the way. Or you could have wanted a girl." Or you could have been on drugs or been an alcoholic or homeless and couldn't manage me."

"My dad said I could always know how much they wanted me because when a person is adopted, they know that their parents have chosen them, it didn't just happen. And he said they always would want me. I believe that. But when I asked them who my "real" parents were, they seemed hurt by my reference to someone else being "real".

"My dad said they didn't know about my birth parents but tried to assure me that he and Mom were my "real" parents even though my mother didn't birth me. My parents said that they got me from the hospital when I was born, and they never saw my parents. I always missed knowing who my birth parents were. Sometimes I would think about it every day but then I felt guilty because Mom and Dad loved me so much and I didn't want to hurt them."

"That was very hard for a young child, wasn't it," Cecily asked.

"Sometimes I'd forget about it for a long time, like years, then something would remind me and my emotions would switch between being angry, bewildered, disconnected...and sometimes happy, that I might have been

146

saved from a bad life. Then I'd think about it every day for a while. When I turned seventeen, I finally told my parents that when I was eighteen I was going to search for you. I told them how much I loved them but that I just had to know my story. They said I didn't have to wait until I was eighteen and that they would help me. I said, 'No I'll wait that long so that I'm done with high school and can spend all my time on the search and be old enough to not need permission to get records. So as soon as I graduated, I went to the county social services office and started the search. My parents always asked about it when I had an interview or received mail and encouraged me, saying that we would find you.

"It's not that I want my life to be different. I love my parents and my sister Julie very much. It's just that, I wish I had known about you and your story, our story. Then I would have been satisfied with how it all turned out."

"Bobby, I don't know where to begin, but I'll try. I'm very glad that you had a good home. I think you're saying you're confused by my choices and feel I rejected you for some reason you don't understand.

"I'm happy you found me. I wanted so badly for many years, to find you. I looked every way I knew how after you were born, but finally I accepted what everyone was telling me, that I would only disrupt a happy family if I did find you.

147

Maybe I shouldn't have accepted that but it was different then and I have to accept that people thought they were doing the best thing for everyone involved. Adoptions used to be kept secret so that the new parents and children could bond with each other and not feel fragmented, belonging in two places.

"Anyway, here's my story.

"I was only fifteen when I got pregnant and sixteen when you were born. I wanted to keep you so badly, but I wasn't mature enough to know how to handle the situation. I remember that you were the most beautiful baby ever born. You were perfect. Everyone told me you looked just like me. And when the doctor held you up, as soon as you could breathe you burst into such a loud cry that all of the nurses and the doctor laughed at you. And they let me try to breast feed you just one time. And Bobby, that was the only time I ever saw you. I was devastated the next morning when I learned you were already gone from the hospital."

Cecily was careful to avoid blaming her loss on her parents although she would probably never lose the pain she felt from what she still thought, was deceit. It was important that Bobby be able to love them.

After some time, trying to hang on to the details he had never known about himself, Bobby asked,

"Who is my dad?" Didn't he want me or want to marry you?"

"Your dad also was fifteen. What I have to tell you now will be hard for you to understand but I hope you can give yourself some time and try to understand. I want you to know only the truth and only as much truth as you want to handle. Once you're ready, only if you want to, we can see if we can have some DNA testing done and identify your dad."

"You mean you don't know who my dad is? Bobby asked. "Were you a prostitute?"

"No Bobby, I was not a prostitute and you were conceived in love, but it was a fifteen-year-old kind of love. You've met my parents now and seen my home. You must realize that it was a good and caring home. Know too, that I was a good and caring kind of girl. I was an only child and my parents wanted me to have friends, someone close to me. They welcomed everyone and I think it left me with no inhibitions. But, about your father.

"The summer I was fifteen I went on a camping trip with the teens from my church. It was cool at night and after full days of swimming, fishing, boating and games we would cook around a bonfire, share our food and sing songs. Then we would all get sleepy and eventually go off to our tents. I had a small tent. I had it all to myself the last few days

149

because my tent mate got homesick and sent for her parents to come for her. One of the last nights after we turned in it started raining and thundering. One of the boys stuck his head in my tent to see if I was okay. He was a kind and fun guy I liked a lot. He impressed me when I saw how good he was to another boy that had a stutter and was laughed at by some of the others and was usually alone.

"So, I said, 'Yeah, I'm okay, but come on in and listen to the rain with me.' So he came in and sat by me. I was shivering in the cold. He put his arm around me to warm me up and we talked quietly and kind of cuddled. Then we got turned on and kissed and then we climbed into my sleeping bag to get warmer. We really didn't have sex in mind, but before you know it, it was so exciting for us that until we almost couldn't stop. It was the first sex experience for both of us. I hadn't even kissed a boy before that, except once a little peck when I was ten years old."

"The next day his good friend came with him to sit by me at the campfire. I said to him, 'Do you want to come back tonight?' He said, "Could my friend (the one with the stutter) be with you tonight in my place?' I knew I should say 'no' and actually, I did. But that night after we turned in, there was his friend sneaking into my tent. This time I didn't say 'no' like I should have. I was feeling sorry for him. After

150

cuddling up for a while we were both so ready. After that, the next day I told them both, 'No more. We shouldn't be doing this. We don't even have any condoms or anything because we never thought it would happen when we were just having fun together.'

Cecily kept telling her story factually as if she had no emotion attached to it while Bobby's eyes widened and his mouth opened wide, dumbfounded by his own life's story.

"So, you see both of them were acts of love, in a way, but not the kind of love that was ready for a lifelong commitment or for child raising responsibilities. When I found out I was pregnant I never told either of the guys I had slept with because I didn't want to ruin their lives with guilt feelings or the responsibility. They must have guessed what happened when I left town, but neither of them came forward. I refused to tell anyone else what happened either. My parents and the medical and social workers tried to pry the information out of me, but I never gave in.

"If both of them are all still living and can be reached, I would be willing now to speak with them about having DNA tests. Times are different now and we are all adult. I'll bet your father would be willing, maybe happy to find out about you. You can let me know how you feel about that after you have some time to think about it. You may want to ask your parents what they think about that too. They can help you decide.

"Bobby, I'm not sure I understand exactly why my parents were so opposed to me raising you. It might help you to know, that they lost a son themselves, when he was five days old. My parents were older and were too devastated to try again. That might have had something to do with their reaction to my pregnancy. Maybe they were afraid that I couldn't handle it if something happened to my child. They are good people. I have to have compassion for them and know that they made the best decision for you and me that they could at the time.

"My other option may have been an abortion, but they wouldn't have liked that either. They never suggested it and I would have fought the suggestion anyway."

"I'm glad you didn't do that," Bobby said. "If I hadn't been born and then adopted I would never have had a little sister Julie. I love Julie so much and she has needed a big brother. But I don't know how to feel about the rest of this. Being raised by you and your parents would have saved me all the confusion and loneliness I've experienced. On the other hand, I am who I am because of the family who raised me not because of you, and I like being who I am.

"What I said my dad told me, that adoptive parents get to choose their children, well I think its the same for us kids, we get to choose our parents. I absolutely, positively already know my choice. My parents are and will always be Robert and Rebecca Ainsley.

"No, I don't wish I had you for a mom instead. Your story doesn't really fit with who I think I am. I'm sorry if I can't call you mother. I'm doing my best to accept you and the facts, but don't try too hard to be a part of my everyday life. You and your parents will probably just be friendly acquaintances, distant relatives. I had to know who you are, but I can't do more than that."

Cecily's heart beat fast as she searched for some idea of a way to hold on to Bobby. First her search, then her longing for Bobby had shaped her adult life. Apparently, he couldn't care what it had done to her and her parents. He was grateful now for the way it had shaped his life. What if, after this week he'd be gone. He wouldn't need her. So, this is how it would be now. No Bobby, nothing to hope for. It was like her life and his had been fiction, not even real.

"I can see how much you loved and wanted me," he said, "but trying to pay you back what I owe you would be too unsettling for me. I can never be grateful enough for life, which you gave me, and for letting me go when I was a baby.

153

Then, please, find your peace in letting me go again, now, and know I am grateful for that too."

Her lower lip twitched as she desperately tried to hold back her tears. All of her dreams of this day were ended in this one conversation. But she had to let him go, pretend he was just a casual acquaintance, a very mature one. She grabbed and hugged him and held her voice steady long enough to say, "It's okay Bobby. It's your decision." Then she swallowed and maintained her composure while she asked, "Are you ready to go back to the house?"

"No," Bobby said, "I'd like to walk around the farm alone, a little longer. Can we talk some more later?"

"Of course, we can. We will talk about everything that you want to know, and no more than you want. I want you to have all your questions answered." Cecily said, "and Bobby, you don't have to call me 'Mom'. Rebecca Ainsley is your mother. You can call me 'Cecily.' But know that I do, and will always love you as a son," she added then turned and walked alone back toward the house alone.

When she arrived at the house, there was Rainbird's truck in the front driveway. She was so afraid to go into her home, not wanting her parents to see the devastation in her eyes, so she climbed in the truck and waited for Rainbird to return to it. When he saw her sitting there with that controlled look of despair on her face he jumped in and without a word, took her in his arms. "Do you want to tell me?" he asked.

"Later," she answered. "Just drive around for a while."

It was two hours later when Cecily returned to her kitchen where her mom's pumpkin bread was waiting for her on the kitchen table. By that time her eyes were no longer red and Rainbird gladly shared the burden with her. He jumped down from the truck. "Do you want to tell your mom about it now or later?" he asked.

"She's going to ask, 'how did it go?' and I have to say something."

"You'll know what to say," he answered.

* * * * *

Cecily and Bobby never did have a further conversation about his life, his parenting, his choices. It seemed to be a settled and closed topic for him. He knew who he was and who he wasn't. He made the decision that he would not investigate his father. "I look like Grandpa Wally," he laughed. That's good enough for me." It was Cecily who didn't know who she was now.

Chapter 18

Jahanara

2017

Within the week after Thanksgiving, Cecily and her parents and Aubrey's Uncle Oscar and Aunt Charlotte were due in Tennessee for her best friend Aubrey's wedding to Aida. This beautiful all-inclusive community focused wedding was enough to re-focus her thoughts from all of the pain and self-pity she would otherwise have been experiencing after her decisive conversation with Bobby.

Cecily followed the yellow rose petals strewn by Aubrey and Aida's adopted child, Jahanara, as the child and Cecily's dog, Romeo led the wedding procession. All of them, dressed in variations of pink and yellow, were followed by the bride Aida as they processed across the Ocoee River bridge.

Aida wore Aubrey's gift, the hand fashioned pink and yellow Thai silk that he had been gifted in Thailand. It graced her head and shoulders like a hijab.

When the wedding ceremony and celebration were over, thinking that Cecily would be leaving for Seaside the next day, Aubrey knew he had to find time to talk with her about her experience with Bobby. He found her sitting at his computer and suggested they walk out into his yard for a talk. Cecily instantly closed the computer and jumped up from her chair.

"I feel like an Olympic star must feel," she started, as they headed outside to the bench under the Willow tree. "Olympians spend their entire childhood working toward that gold. They give up friends, fun times, sleep. They endure pain in their drive toward perfection. Their whole family sometimes moves to another town in order to be near their coach who works with them for hours every day over the years. They study with a private tutor because it is impossible to maintain their practice schedule and hours of public school at the same time. By age sixteen they may make it to the Olympics but do not win the gold. They keep trying. Then one year they win. The gold medal is around their neck and the world cheers for ten minutes. Then they go home and now what? They have time on their hands and no higher aim than what they've already reached. Everything else seems like downhill from that gold.

"I have reached my goal, Aubrey. I wear the gold coin, my Bobby, around my neck. Now what? I feel like the gold coin will be a heavy weight. He is not really mine as I had dreamt he would be. He belongs to Rebecca and Robert and Julie. I cannot live the rest of my life in his shadow, jumping at every chance I have to be with him nor can I ask that of him...now what?"

"Cecily, now you begin to live. Now you can experience the now that you are living in. Now you can move to where you want to live, change jobs if you see fit, be closer to your parents, maybe fall in love again. Now you can live Cecily's life, not Bobby's mother's life."

"I will always regret..."

"No regrets, Cecily. Learn from your parents how to love your present. Don't you think they have felt regret over how they handled the situation twenty years ago? Of course they have but they're going forward and are so happy to have you. Still, your parents will say goodbye to you and send you back to Seaside with an ache in their heart, tears in their eyes, but a dance in their step because you were here."

"Then I am to return home to Seaside and get to work again and keep wishing I was someplace else…"

"Cecily, test it. Test happiness. Practice being care-free."

"How do I do that?"

"It will be hard at first. You might even feel guilty being free of your gold weight, but this is the time to live and cele-brate the growth you missed out on since you were sixteen. Life owes this to you now. When your parents invite you for Christmas, jump in your truck and go. If Rainbird calls with a story of some difficulty, offer to come and help him. When your staff says you should take the day off, do it. Invite Ja-hanara and Aida and Me to your home. After experiencing freedom for a while you will know where you belong and you'll have your own new goals. Your new medal will be plat-inum, it will not be downhill from the gold you already have. It will be the best time of your life, you will see."

The wind was picking up and the willow needles brushed her face. "Aubrey, I love you so much. You always know what to say to me. Thank you for this time. But now, go find Aida. I think she's waiting for you up in your bedroom where she's pretending to be all involved with packing a suit-case. I'm going to find Jahanara and have her tell me all about herself. I need her version of adopted life. That may help me get a little closer to Bobby's perspective of his life. She can be my counselor."

Cecily found four-year-old Jahanara sitting on the front porch step playing with her doll. She jumped up when she saw Cecily coming. Cecily said, "Let's go find some stumps to sit on. I want to talk to you about life."

"Okay. What is life?"

"You know that dead gecko you showed me? Well, it used to have life before it got hurt and then it died. It used to run around and eat and look at you with big wide-open eyes. That is life. When it lost its life it couldn't do those things any more."

"I can run around and eat and look at you, so I have life," Jahanara said.

"Yes, with your life you can do many more things than the gecko. You can think and talk and laugh and tell stories and love your mom and dad…"

"And you," she interrupted.

"Yes, you can love me too.

"And your Grandma Alia and many more people and even Romeo."

She thought about that.

"Can I love my dead mom that doesn't have life?" Jahanara asked.

"Yes, you can love her too. Do you remember your dead mom, Jahanara?" I asked since she had given me the perfect opening.

"Yes?" she said, her tone sounding more like a question than answer. "She was very beautiful...And she had very good friends, but they couldn't keep me when she died so she gave me to my new mom. And she said my new mom could give me a name. I know my new mom loves me because my name is always safe in her mouth."

"What did your first mom call you?" I asked her.

"I think my name from my first mom was 'Thekid," she said.

She thought about what she had said for a minute, then added, "I'm glad she gave me to my new mom. She's very pretty too. And now I have a daddy too. I never had a daddy before."

Then Jahanara giggled.

"What's funny?" I asked.

"Now I'm getting fat too. My daddy calls me 'Hammy' like a piggy because pigs are fat too. He said I used to be skinny, but now I eat so much. He says he likes me to be fat. If he picks me up every day while I'm getting fat he will still be able to pick me up when I'm as big as a elephant."

"It sounds like you love your daddy," I said.

"Yes. And he loves me too. He even said so." She thought for a while, then, satisfied with her concept of life, reached down and picked up her doll and looked at it a little sadly. "I love you anyway, even if you don't have life, Susie," she said to the doll. "Because you make me smile when I'm tired and then we go to sleep together."

"Do you like school, Jahanara," I asked next.

"Oh yes, but it's not real school, it's just a play school called day care. My day care lady's name is Sammie. Sammie says I'm smart, but I know too many words. There's some words she told me to forget."

"What words are those?" I asked.

Jahanara pulled me down by the shoulder to whisper in my ear. "Don't tell my mom I said the words. 'Chit' and 'Fuckin' and 'Bitch'. They're not nice words and I'm a nice girl so I mustn't say them."

"Okay, Jahanara, I won't say those words either and I won't tell your mom. Anyway, you were just explaining to me. You weren't really using the words."

And so I had my first lesson from Jahanara. Could I be as open to life as this child?

Chapter 19

Rainbird

2019

Cecily walked into the warehouse that was now home, sat down on her new recliner, looked around at the room's coldness and called Romeo. He sat in front of her and she put her arms around his neck. When he looked into her eyes she had the sudden feeling that the floor fell through and the earth gave way and she fell through an enormous sink hole to the center of the earth. The feeling came from deeper in her soul than even her loss of Bobby twenty years ago or the loss of her home on the beach. It included all of that.

She finally crawled out of the hole while Romeo waited. She calmed down, but was unable to sleep so she stayed up almost all night unpacking her suitcase and rearranging things in her living space until she finally sat down and dozed off on her recliner. In the morning she awoke early, dressed and headed to her office. She had to get to work. Her sense of shame and dismay would pass once she was busy and felt needed.

She had been away for almost eight weeks, two months, and had a lot of catching up to do. She drew up on her computer, all of the unfinished real estate deals she had been working on when she left for Thanksgiving in Broken Bow. They had all been completed, houses sold, closings scheduled, new clients having been guided in searches. Then she moved over to her travel agency accounts. None pending, deposits or payments in full had been indicated.

"I'm sure my staff worked hard to make this happen," she said out loud to no one. She could hear the staff, "Let's surprise Cecily and have all her pending activity completed. Won't she be happy when gets back and sees she can relax? It'll give her a chance to take some time off and get settled."

And she would have to say to them, "You must have worked hard and you did such a great job. Thank you so much" instead of saying how she really felt: *Coming home to being unneeded makes me feel worse than I already did.*

She went to breakfast at Patty's Wicker Cafe' but had no appetite. She thought she could sit there anyway for a long-time drinking coffee so that she would get back to the office a little late. Then she walked on the boardwalk to soak in some sun and listen to the sound of the waves. She was determined that she would learn to love her place in Seaside again. Then she returned to the office. She gathered the staff in her office and thanked them as planned. Then she said to them, "Thank you so much for the time off that you have provided for me. I will be leaving the office soon for the day as you wanted me to do. I'd like you all to plan a few days off for yourselves now. I know you must have put in lots of overtime even though it was in the middle of the holidays. Please plan to be here tomorrow so that you can go over your work with me and show me what I need to do in your absence, then take the rest of the week off with pay. In your absence I'll work on getting new clients. "

They all cheered, of course, and Cecily had created a win-win. When she left the office, It was 10:30 and the stores were open so she headed to the shops to buy herself a cheer-up present. That idea was a bust though, as each store she entered and all the window shopping, only revealed things she might buy for Dad or Mom or Nicco or Bobby or Aubrey's new family, Jahanara or a baby layette for their expected new baby. She found nothing had any interest for her personally.

Finally, she returned home to get Romeo and took him for a yeoman's walk, through the park, over the new bridge built after the tsunami. They crossed the Necanicum River gushing down from the Humbug Mountain. Then they picked up McDonald hamburgers and had a picnic sitting on the cold hard rocks by the lakeside in Quatat Park. They were back to normal.

When they returned home Cecily texted Nicco telling him that everything was fine and that she was back to normal. She thought he would text her back but in the moment's interlude while she waited for the bamboo sound of a text message the phone rang.

"Hey Cecily, speak to me. I want to hear your voice, not just read your note."

"Rainbird!

"Just talk. Tell me anything at all, just talk."

She rattled off her whole story. She just couldn't stop talking. "It was hard to leave Mom and Dad and I had a good talk with Aubrey before I left, but our drive back was fine and uneventful. When we got back I unpacked and put things away in my new spot in the warehouse then went in to the office early this morning. Then I searched my computer to see what I had left undone so I could get started early, believe it or not my employees had completed all of my work, so I had nothing to do. So I went out for breakfast and took the day off. Then Romeo and I walked all over town and ate burgers in the park. Would you wear a silver Bolo if I bought one for you?"

Rainbird was silent for a minute. He could hear the control in her voice as she rattled on and knew that she was holding back tears. "Cecily would you like me to fly up there to visit you for a few days"

"Oh, Rainbird, you can't do that. I mean, how could you get away?" she asked.

"I can get away for anything as important as this," he said. "Your dad will look after the beasts for me for a few days. I know he will if it would help you."

"It would be so much fun to show you around Seaside. Then in the future when I talk about things I'm doing; you'll know what I'm talking about. Do you really think you can come?"

"I'll be there the day after tomorrow. I'll text you my arrival time as soon as I get it scheduled and you can drive out and pick me up. Be sure you bring Romeo with you."

"Rainbird, how did you know…"

"Cecily I never heard you talk so much without taking a breath. Had to be something wrong."

"I'll be at the airport whenever you say," she said.

"And Cecily, if you want to buy that bolo for me, I'd love to have it."

* * * * *

Rainbird flew into Portland and transferred to a local plane to Seaside so that Cecily wouldn't have to drive two hours to get him. He said he didn't want to waste in transit any of the short time they would have together. She parked in Seaside airport's small parking lot but his plane was early and before she could get out of the car to go inside he was out in front waiting, duffle bag in hand and saw her pull into a parking space. He was at the car in a second and she jumped out and flew into his arms.

"Nicco."

"Cecily," was all they said. They embraced each other so tightly and long that the man in the car next to Cecily's truck started to honk at them. They both jumped, said, "I'm sorry," to him and climbed up into her truck. Nicco threw his duffle bag into the back of the pickup and Romeo sat between them in the front. Niko was wearing a white shirt buttoned all the way up, and a jeans jacket, just the perfect outfit waiting for her gift of a leather rope and silver bolo. They didn't kiss. Although Cecily suddenly felt the urgency of intimacy with Rainbird, her whole body fluttering, they had never discussed an intimate relationship with each other. In fact at one time she had said to Rainbird, "I don't expect I'll ever want to marry. I'm so used to being alone and independent. I'd be pretty hard for someone to live with." And Nicco had said in his vociferous way, "Me too."

I"d better not start something that neither of us will want to continue. I don't want to create an obligation. I don't know how Rainbird was feeling, at the moment. He was probably fluttering too. Such intimacy is not usually something one discusses beforehand. It just happens. Cecily wasn't sure she wanted to let it just happen. Their lives were just too different to be blended and it would be too painful for them to separate once they let it all out.

Cecily brought Nicco to her warehouse-home and set him up in its best room, a second-floor room from which he could see the distant blue of the ocean. Her home even had a freight elevator with an accordion-cage door that made Nicco laugh, "Where is the elevator operator guy?"

"Niko, you're hired if you want the job."

"I'll take the job if you'll marry me," he chuckled.

169

Once he was settled in his room and bathroom which took all of two minutes, Cecily brought him into her office to show him where she would be spending most of her time when life got back to normal. She introduced her staff to him. Then they went to the hospital where both Seamus and Aubrey had worked before the tsunami took its Memory Care Unit and Rehab Unit and most importantly, Seamus. She took Nicco for a drink to the Crazy Frog Saloon and told him the story of Aubrey and his friend Tillie who turned out to be a serial killer. She told him how Romeo had helped Aubrey establish his innocence by finding the box with Tillie's fingerprints on it, after Tillie's attempts to blame him for the murders.

They did a lot of touring on the next three days. She took Nicco to the lighthouse, to the salt works, to the Lewis and Clark exhibition. Together they watched the ocean waves roll in while Rainbird mused about the path and the importance of the ocean in their lives. He said he knew that eventually she would find that even tsunamis were part of the Spirit's care of the earth and all of its people.

The night before he would be leaving, as they sat in her warehouse-living room Rainbird said to Cecily, "There's something about this home that seems right for you at this time. Maybe it's good for you to feel its coldness."

170

"I don't understand what you mean," she answered him.

"It's like warm summer and icy winter, like blossoming trees and bare, wintry skeletons of a tree, it's like beautiful Jahanara and the death of Seamus, it's like the brook bubbling down from the mountain and the painted desert, Cecily. Each of them teaches us. Your warm home on the beach and the cold warehouse where you live now both have something important to teach you. Listen to them. Maybe it's also like the birth of Bobby and your loss of him, or like your wonderful nurse-friend Aubrey and your wild friend, Rainbird.

We, your friends and your parents and this earth will always be there for you. Don't be far away. Don't be afraid. Be close to us. Know love."

She couldn't answer Rainbird. She wished she could have recorded his words but she would try to remember them like she still remembered his words long ago in their childhood when she was leaving home the first time: "The Great Spirit will guide you and your child. I'll wait for you." And it seemed he had waited, but that was twenty years ago, and now it was time for him to go again.

In the morning at the airport before boarding, Nicco Rainbird and Cecily James gave each other a total embrace like the one at the airport parking lot on his arrival, but this time Cecily didn't try to interpret this moment as she had done then. She didn't need to wonder if this was a prelude to sex. It was time for him to return home and sexual intimacy hadn't happened. She didn't have to wonder now. She would see him off and look forward to a next time together without uncomfortably wondering about his intent.

"Please come or call soon. You know, you are always welcome" he said, then placed a kiss on her cheek. He turned to wave as he headed toward the boarding stewardess. As she waved back she suddenly became aware of her own emptiness and she shivered.

She was like the bud of a sunflower, trying, on the verge, of bursting into a glorious yellow blossom. *How long will she be on the verge?* Rainbird wondered. *Will a flower eventually wither and die if not allowed to blossom?*

Chapter 20

Evelyn and Wally

2020

Near Easter the next year, Evelyn called Cecily and asked, "would you like to come and visit us for Easter? I don't want to put any pressure on you. I know you are busy with work, but I want you to know you're welcome."

"Mom, why don't you and Dad come here for Easter? I'd love to have you and you've never been to Seaside to see where I live."

"That's a wonderful idea," Evelyn said. "Let me talk to your father. He's outside right now but I'll call you back as soon as we discuss it"

It wasn't two minutes later that she called back. "We'd love to come to Seaside, Cecily. We'll ask Mr. Rainbird to help us with plane reservations since he's been there recently. He can call and let you know when we're arriving."

Cecily could hear Wally saying, "Ask her about the weather…and how long does she think we should stay."

"Tell Dad you can stay as long as you like, but in about a week you can see everything there is to see here. It's winter here too, you know, so there won't be much sitting on the beach or anything like that. But I have plenty of room, and," she said, "Tell Dad I'll ask Romeo to give up his bed for him."

Evelyn and Wally arrived in Seaside for the first time ever on the day before Easter with plans to stay for a week. Cecily toured them all around the same places she had taken Nicco and she took them to town with her to shop. Dad wanted to buy a gift for Rainbird to thank him "for looking after my daughter." He bought him salt-licks for his sheep, woodchuck, cattle deer, tqpir, fox and moose. The salt had been harvested from the Pacific Ocean. It was a twenty-pound addition to Dad's return trip luggage.

The last morning of their stay Cecily asked them, "What would you like to do today since it's the last day of your first time here?

Her mom answered, "Cecily you've shown us where you live now and where you work now, and the new bridge and some new hotels and restaurants. I want to see where

174

everything used to be, how it was for you here before the tsunami? If it's not too hard for you, I'd like to see where you worked when you were in school, where you used to live, used to work. It would help me understand you."

Her dad said, "Hush, Evelyn. It might be too hard for her, just reminding her of things she lost."

Cecily saw in their eyes their pain but also their willingness to bear the cost at their own expense rather than hurt her. She knew that she had to do this, what she had been avoiding all week. She remembered Rainbird's words to her that day in the truck five months ago when he asked her, "Do you know what 'hush now' means to your Dad? It means there's nothing to forgive. But there will be a time..."

This was the time. "I want very much to show you those things and those places," she said to them. "Let's start by driving down to the beach where my house used to be and I'll tell you all about it."

And as she did she started to understand Nicco's words to her. Standing with her parents looking out at the ocean over the empty beach where her home had been was like rebuilding that little house for them to see. As she tried to help them see its beauty, she felt proud of what she had accomplished there. The sea that drowned her home had also drowned her loneliness, her distance from them and others, her need to punish her parents. The waters of the tsunami were finally filling her emptiness.

* * * * *

Bobby had decided he didn't care about searching any further for his father. Although their families had gotten to know and like each other during the week they spent together after Aubrey and Aida's wedding, their togetherness had been an effort. Their only communication since then had been a few emails to say "Thank You", "Merry Christmas" and to give her notice of Bobby's graduation from The Art Institute in Chicago. Their notes were polite and gracious but not inviting.

The next summer, Cecily drove with Romeo to Oklahoma again. This time she gave total responsibility to the staff of her two businesses so that she could be gone for a two month stretch again. Aubrey, Aida, Jahanara and Seamus the new baby came for two weeks. Jahanara was a natural with the animals already at the age of six. Though the family was staying with Aubrey's Aunt and Uncle, they allowed Jahanara to stay with Cecily at Nicco's place every day until being among the animals almost felt like home to her. And with Seamus two years old, Aida was pregnant again.

Cecily's mom was eighty years old now, and her dad a few years older. They were both thriving. Nicco had become like a son to them. Because of Nicco's help Wally was able to continue caring for his few sheep. Maybe it was time for Cecily to move back to Oklahoma.

Chapter 21

The Gentiles

2020

"Cecily, this is Pari calling from Tennessee. I'm the aunt of your friends, Aida and Aubrey."

"Yes, I know who you are, Pari. What's going on?" Cecily asked, wondering why Pari and not Aida or Aida's mother would be calling. *Maybe they're having a baby shower for Aida's third child. Or maybe Aida's mother, Alia is sick. Or maybe there's a surprise planned for... something and they want me to come. The baby is due soon, maybe it's going to be premature.*

The wait was too long before Pari could speak again.

"Is there something wrong, Pari?

"I'm so sorry," Pari said and broke into sobbing, couldn't say anymore.

Cecily grabbed a kitchen chair and sat down, realizing suddenly that this call was going to be a bad news call.

Finally, Pari got it out. "Something terrible has happened to Aida. She was working on a revision of the landscaping below the dam in Blue Ridge when the dam broke, and she was swept away in the water.

"Oh my God, no, Pari. Is she okay? And the baby?

"Aida might not make it.

"The baby is going to be okay, I think. They did a Cesarian as soon as they got Aida to the hospital and they're keeping the baby in ICU for observation. She's already five pounds big."

" I'll be right there as soon as I can get a flight out of here. I know you all must need some help. How is Aubrey? How are the children?"

"Aubrey is staying at the hospital, won't leave Aida's side, of course. I'm staying at their house with Jahanara and Seamus and Aida's mom Alia goes back and forth."

"You tell Aubrey that I'll be there tomorrow. And Pari, don't worry about anyone picking me up at the airport. I'll figure it out when I get there and find a ride to the hospital myself."

"Oh Cecily, I'm so glad you can come. It will help Aubrey so much. And by the way, Aida wanted to name the baby after you, Jasmine for her favorite flower and Cecelia for you. Jasmine Cecelia. Is that okay with you?"

Cecily immediately called Nicco to tell him what had happened. "I don't know what to do about Romeo," she said.

"Cecily, Ask your staff to feed and walk him until I get there. I will fly out on the first plane I can get. I'll pick him up and drive with him back here in your truck. Then you can come straight here to Broken Bow when you are ready to leave Aubrey. He may need you for a while."

"I have no idea how long I will be in Tennessee," she said.

"Ceci, Aubrey needs you now."

"Oh, and Rainbird, the new baby is named after me," she said with a broken voice and tears that were too happy and too sad at once to be reconciled.

Cecily informed the managers of her two offices who were now very capable of doing without her. "I don't know when I'll be back," she said, "so just run this place like it's your own business.

"Do I get to keep Romeo for you?" her manager Marilyn asked.

"Only for a day or two, til Rainbird gets here."

"Oh, that lucky Rainbird," she smiled. All of her staff were well acquainted with Rainbird now.

* * * * *

After Aida died Aubrey was like a snowman melting in the sun. He tried to return to work believing that work would help him forget, but it was quite the opposite for him as his work was nursing and everyday brought him reminders of the loss he was trying to forget. Jahanara was seven years old now and Seamus only three. Although Jahanara could not remember her birth mother, Aida had told her all about Jocelyn, her mother. Now she was learning that mothers left you, you couldn't count on having a mother, you had to be strong. Aubrey took a leave of absence from work for the rest of the school year and into the summer to be with the children and to help himself face the future without Aida.

Cecily stayed on in Tennessee trying her best to be a substitute mother to the children. And, Aida's mother Alia and aunt Pari also moved into the little house. They all worked at rearranging the house and blend their "families". Pari and Alia used the guest bedroom. Cecily, now had opened up the day bed that was in the office. The two older children shared a room and Aubrey insisted on keeping the baby with him and being the one to get up with her during the night.

As the new school year approached, Aubrey returned to work and moved the baby in with her grandmother, Alia. He was back to working twelve-hour shifts which enabled him to be home with the children four days a week. Cecily had been with Aubrey and his family almost six months. Her daily phone conversations with Nicco had dwindled to weekly.

One Sunday in the middle of a less than enthused conversation Nicco finally said to her, "Cecily, I will under-stand if you think you need to stay with Aubrey and the chil-dren now. You and Aubrey have been lifelong friends and you've been through a lot together. Please know that you are free for him if that is what you want. I will not stand in your way."

Cecily gasped and shook her head. Though Rainbird couldn't see her he knew exactly how that looked. "Rainbird, I hadn't thought about "being in love with Aubrey. If it seems like that's the reason I've stayed here so long, it's not true. I just think Aubrey needs me for the children," she said.

"Does he Cecily?"

Nicco waited cooly for her to make a clearer statement, to say, 'yes, I'm in love with Aubrey,' or to say, 'no Rainbird, I'm in love with you.' But she couldn't and didn't say either.

"Cecily, I have to hang up now. Please think about this and do what is best for you all," he finally said.

That evening when Aubrey returned from work the children waited by the door and jumped into his arms the minute the door opened as they always did now. Jahanara was wearing a new cotton plaid dress. "See what Grandma Alia bought me for my first day of school," she told him proudly.

Aubrey picked her up. "What happened to my Hammy?" he asked. "You are growing tall and slender and sturdy like your Mom. And now you will be in third grade. I love you so much." He put her down and said, "Little J., let's go upstairs and you can help me put Seamus to bed. You can read his airplane book to him for me."

"Okay Daddy, like Mamma used to do?"

"Aubrey, I'll read to the children if you wish," Cecily interrupted.

"No Cecily, I promised Aida that I would read to them at night. Even if Aida could not hear me make that promise when she was in a coma, I must do that for her. It was always a time when she felt very close to them. It's a family thing. Only Jahanara can take her place."

When both children had gone to bed and Alia and Pari, having put baby Jasmine to bed as well, were in the kitchen cutting oranges and shredding a coconut for Harissah, Cecily followed Aubrey out onto the porch and sat down next to him on the swing. She snuggled up to him and reminisced. "Remember sitting on my porch swing in Seaside when you first came back from Thailand?"

"I was just remembering being on this swing in the dark with Aida. This is where I proposed to her," Aubrey said.

Cecily hoped he couldn't see her face fall as she looked away from him. "I am intruding, aren't I?" she said.

"Cecily, I think it's time for you to leave us," Aubrey said.

"But the children. You won't have time to get them off to school in the morning and Alia can't stay here forever. And Aubrey, who will take care of you emotionally if I am gone? I know I can't replace Aida, but I think you need a woman in your life."

"Cecily it's not the children keeping you here. Alia is their grandmother and she is the best person to care for them. And Pari, too, is helping. Are you trying to get some of the closeness back that you and I had when I lived with you?

You know, you were never in love with me. Even when I lived with you in Seaside we never developed a romantic interest.

"I think we were testing it, but as soon as Aida arrived in my life I knew the difference. It was as glaring as a trumpet blast. I was in love with Aida like I had never been in love with you...except maybe when we were ten. When I met Aida I suddenly found myself dressing as I thought she would like, even when she wasn't there. When I laughed at a joke, I couldn't wait to tell her the joke, I called her to tell her what I had to eat. I gave up a job that I loved to be near her. Aida and I couldn't wait to complete each other. We didn't have to figure out if this was the right person for us.

"I will always be grateful to you for helping me find Aida. Your love for me now is more like either pity or responsibility. You are not in love with me, Cecily."

"But we enjoy each other. Aida would want you to be happy again."

"Cecily, a part of me lies below the Blue Ridge dam. A part of me is under our willow tree in the backyard where Aida planted the Jasmine. And a part of me is in Alia and Seamus and Jahanara and baby Jasmine.

"Yes Aida would want me to be happy and someday I may fall in love again. But you belong in Oklahoma. You belong to your parents and maybe to Rainbird."

"Rainbird and I..."

"I know, you're going to say Rainbird isn't right for you. Is that why you learned to hand feed baby goats and pick horses hooves? Is that why you laugh so hard when you tell me about Rainbird and his dog sharing peanuts in the shell, or Rainbird helping your dad pull the lamb from the ewe? How often during each day do you think of him? Who did you call first to talk about finding Bobby? Who did you tell first about Aida's accident? Is all of that because you're in love with me?

"Cecily, Rainbird adores you, so much that he's willing to let you go if that's what you and I want. But it's not what he wants.

"And anyway, I need you to be in Oklahoma. Jahanara needs you there too, so she can visit you and the broken animals."

Aubrey looked kindly into Cecily's eyes, drew her close for a bear hug and kissed her on the forehead. She sat back in the swing, gave it a few pushes putting it into motion with her foot and then took his hand. She looked up at him and nodded but was unable to say anything. This was his answer. She knew he was right; she had never been in love with him. It was only that she had begun to hope that his need would give her a *raison d'etre.* She put the break on the swing with her foot and got up and walked alone into the house.

The kitchen was smelling of coconut and Pari was pulling the last cake from the oven.

"Do you think you could give me a crash baking course in the next day or two?" she asked the women. My friend Nicco and my parents will love it if I can bake kunafah for them when I get home." She would truly miss Middle Eastern cooking, especially their desserts. Chicken soup just didn't compare to kunafah, shaabiyat, baklava, semolina cake or harissah.

They both looked surprised at her question then glanced at each other with careful nods of relief. "Of course, we can," they said almost in unison. "We start cooking and baking class first thing tomorrow morning."

As soon as Cecily got to her room, Aubrey's office that she had turned into a bedroom for herself, she called Rainbird. "I'm coming home," she said.

"Are you coming to my house?" he asked."

"Yes, if you'll have me," she answered.

"Oh, Cecily, of course I'll have you. I've missed you so much. I'm like a monkey without a tail to swing from without you." Then he added cautiously, "Will you be staying a while, or will you need to get back to the children?"

"No, I won't be going back to Aubrey," she answered.

"And what about your job?" he asked.

"Guess I'll have to get back to Seaside eventually," she said, unsure of what to do about Seaside. "We need to talk about that though."

In the morning Cecily called her parents. "I'm coming home," she said excitedly.

"Oh honey, I know," her mom said. "Nicco called us at ten o'clock last night. He couldn't wait to tell us. He has already gone over to Jerry's Farm to get a turkey. He wants me to make a Thanksgiving dinner for your arrival day."

Two mornings later Nicco called Wally. "The ship has sailed," he said. She arrives in Texarkana at noon. Tell Evelyn that she can have the turkey ready for about four o'clock. I'll bring the yams and cranberries and pumpkin pie."

Chapter 22

Rainbird

2020

Cecily boarded her plane with sadness in her heart. She knew that Aubrey had been right. She was not in love with him, only sad for him, and she could not fill his empty soul. Nor hers. When Aida died it was like Aubrey's spirit had drifted off into the wind like Aida's silk scarf, leaving his empty body to navigate life. But Aubrey was navigating, he was filling his life again, not with Cecily but with the family that was his life, Aida's family. Cecily mused, but not for long, on Jahanara reading to little Seamus, Alia raising Jasmine.

Now she could also see Rainbird waiting for her plane. Was that excitement she was feeling, hardly recognizing?

Was the warmth that began seeping in to fill her sad soul, from the prospect of seeing Rainbird again? Or was it from the prospect of her mom's oven roasting a thanksgiving turkey? The kitchen of her childhood home was filled with warmth and the aroma of buoyant contentment.

As her Beech18 descended through the white fluffy clouds and she looked down at the Oklahoma landscape, it was her almost certain vision of Nicco Rainbird that made her heart flutter.

When she landed, he was there waiting as she knew he would be. Nicco held back hesitantly as she walked toward him but Cecily ran, her suitcase hitting against her ankles until she buried herself in his arms and inhaled the hay. She reached for his cheeks with her two hands and smoothed his neat, short, thick, brown beard with her two thumbs and found his lips.

No questions were asked about Aubrey or her relationship with him, nor would there ever be for he knew the answer. He reached for her suitcase with his left hand and for her hand with his right. She knew with certainty now, Nicco Rainbird was not a default.

He wasn't just the buddy that she had gone hiking with and laughingly hidden from, beneath the ivy on the mountain trail when they were fifteen. He was now strong but gentle.

He was warm and affectionate but still distant like he was afraid of getting too close to her, afraid of forcing himself on her or maybe afraid of losing her again.

After her return, Cecily spent most of her days with Rainbird, learning to care for his broken animals. They headed each day at dinner time to her parents' house where her mother had been cooking like it was Thanksgiving every day, she was so happy to have them to cook for. Then Nicco would return home and Cecily would sleep at her parents' house, heading back to Rainbird's after breakfast.

Cecily was learning to love Oklahoma and many things about it. She had never lived there as an adult. Her time with Rainbird and his family when they were kids had been the closest, she had ever come to appreciating the peace and beauty of the area. Now she saw the yellow fields of black eyed Susan's and purple, red and blue wildflowers, all blowing east or west at the same time like a flock of birds who sit together, facing the same direction. Where were the flowers when she was a teen and wanted only to get away?

She also had never had an uninhibited adult relationship with her parents, and she didn't know quite how. Her parents were this amazing couple standing between two worlds. They were like a bridge from the peaceful, thriving, hopeful post second world war era to the parenthood of a damaged daughter who yet was like a new baby to them. They wanted to give her constant attention and she felt guilty setting limits.

Cecily was lying in bed one morning musing about a dream in which all of these elements took shape. In her dream a huge frightening rabbit chased her as she ran. Whenever he got near to her he suddenly hid from her. Then she started to fly upward and away from the rabbit but was restricted by something tied to her foot. Then she saw that it was her mother's apron strings wrapped around her foot. The rabbit suddenly turned into Seamus, her fiancé' who tried to rescue her but she flew beyond his reach. Then Aubrey showed up and tried to cut the apron string, but it wouldn't cut. Then Nicco chased her, caught her by the foot and pulled her down but then turned and started to walk away. And she was left standing alone, bewildered.

Suddenly she was awakened by the phone.

"Cecily, ready for a day in the mountains?" It was Rainbird.

"Now?"

"Yep. As soon as you can get ready."

"But the animals."

"Your dad is already here. He wants to take care of the animals for me so you and I can have a day off. He'll take care of Romeo too."

"Oh, well that's a surprise. Oh, okay. I'll come over and cook up some breakfast and make sandwiches for lunch."

"Now you're sounding like your mom. I love your mom, but don't turn into her yet. Just get dressed and I'll be there in fifteen."

Cecily jumped up from the bed, made the bed as she always did, it was a compulsion, ran into and out of the shower, dried off and pulled on her navy short shorts, red tee, sandals, and pulled her blond ponytail through the Velcro strap of her red baseball cap. She threw jeans, socks, tennies and a sweater in a grocery store reusable bag just in case, not knowing what Rainbird had in mind for the day.

She was waiting out in front of the house when Rainbird's truck pulled up in front. Except for his jeans, they looked like they had planned their twin-like outfits.

Cecily jumped into the passenger seat as Rainbird was slapping his knees to the rhythm of Country Western music. He turned off the radio.

"Where are we going? She asked.

"To our spot."

"Oh?" she said.

"Something about this seems like deja vu.

"Rainbird, do you remember driving up there together the day…"

"You mean the day you told me you were pregnant Cecily? How could I forget?"

"It seems like you've always been right here for me every time I'm in trouble or have a crisis of some sort, Nicco. You must be getting tired of my crises. I'm sure you must want to run when you see it's me on the phone. I need to start calling on you when my life is going great."

"Cecily, on the contrary. When I see it's you calling my heart does this little jitterbug thingy and I grab the phone as fast as I can before you hang up.

"That's what today is about. We're here to have fun together. No problems allowed.

"I brought my hibachi grill to cook breakfast if you're hungry. We have brook trout, eggs, your mom's biscuits and coffee. First thing, let's go to "our place" and eat breakfast there."

"Nicco, I'm starved."

After breakfast Cecily said, looking up at Rainbird, "Nicco, I want to climb that Norfolk pine tree. Remember how little it was when we used to come up here? Still, even then, we could see the entire Red River Valley from up in the tree, even further than we could see from our rock overlook."

"I remember."

Cecily went first. Each time she reached a new branch level he pulled himself up behind her putting his open hand on her buns and saying, "Oh, sorry, accident," as he chuckled. She laughed too but by the time she reached the third branch level she had to stop, to sit on it. Nicco followed. Sat down beside her. The branch was so strong it hardly moved with his weight. By the time he put his hand on her thigh, her heart was pulsating. Her hands were vibrating. Her legs were throbbing. Her pelvis was fluttering. Her voice was silent, couldn't utter a sound.

She leaned into Nicco, trembling. "I didn't expect this," she said, but Nicco…" she looked up into his eyes, unable to say any more.

"Hush now," Nicco said smiling as he put his arms about her securely, took her chin into his strong hand and kissed her softly, gently on the mouth, then looked into her eager eyes, studied them once more.

"Nicco, I can't…wait any longer," Cecily said as she grabbed his head with her free hand while hanging onto the higher branch with the other hand. She kissed him back, with all her strength and all her breath. Longingly. Lastingly. Desperately.

"No more waiting, Cecily" he managed to whisper while catching his breath, then smiled ever so slightly, "but I think we better get out of the tree. Not a good place for what's coming."

Rainbird held on to Cecily as he started to climb down without losing the heat of the moment. She could barely move off the branch behind him, didn't even notice how the bark of the tree scraped her thighs as she slid recklessly down to the ground.

"Cecily, I have blankets in the car that I can spread out by the fire, but are you sure you want to do this?"

"Nicco, I've never been so sure. Finally. I'm a slow learner but...oh, just hurry."

He pulled the blankets from the truck and spread them by the fire. "Cecily, Let me help you," he said as he started by pulling off her cap **and** loosening her pony tail. "I want to see you with the sun on you."

Their hiking never went any further that morning. They stayed in their own place behind the rock that overlooked the valley, beneath the massive Norfolk pine that they had loved even when it was young." Eventually they fell asleep together under a light blanket on ground dappled by sun-shine with a slight breeze barely rustling the trees.

When they awoke the sun had reached its up high two o'clock position.

"Cecily let's take a hike. I want to remember this day forever. It's too soon for us to go home. Let's explore some direction we haven't been before."

"Remember, Nicco, how your dad would never let us rock climb. We always wanted to climb after rock climbing became sort of a fad and our friends were climbing. Let's do it now."

Chapter 23

The Climb

2020

"Don't be so eager, Cecily. My dad was a wise man. It's dangerous if you don't know what you're doing." Rainbird. We won't go very high. You can show me how."

"I have some gear in the truck that I keep there in case I ever have to rescue an animal in the mountains."

"Do we need gloves?"

"My gloves won't fit you but you'll have to wear them or your hands will be in shreds by the time we're done. You know Cecily, I don't have much experience with this."

"Oh, we can do it Rainbird. I want to see the valley from up there."

"I think we'll be safe if we find a gently pitched rock and don't go very high. I think I have two harnesses and some cams and a crash pad in case one one of us falls.

"I'm going first," Rainbird said after he showed Cecily the equipment and how each piece works. I'll go a few feet, attach the rope around a secure part of the rock and then help you up to me. Then if that goes okay, I'll climb a few more feet the same way. We're only going up that small cliff, no higher the first time. He pointed to a rock about twenty-five feet high with a protuberance that jutted out over a bubbling brook and seemed to have lots of foot holds. "Our lunch is in my backpack so we won't need to carry anything else. We'll just sit on that rock and have lunch and then climb back down."

Ragged hands, hoarse from screaming to each other and torn tees later they swung their feet over the edge of the rock feeling muscle sore, but happy to be successful and safe. Rainbird pulled the lunch he had brought from his backpack. "I wasn't worried about our nutrition for one day. Just packed good stuff," he said. Lunch consisted of potato chips, pretzels, peanuts, and cherry pie.

"How do we descend?" Cecily asked after the sweat from their climb had dried off in the northern breeze.

"Same way we climbed up. I go first in case you fall. I'll catch you."

"Right. Then we both fall and there's no one else here to rescue us."

Rainbird donned his gloves, threw his looped rope around a sturdy rock outcropping and hanging on to it, dangled his body over the edge. His feet landed securely about five feet from the top. "Now you," he called. Cecily looked down at him. "I'm scared," she said trembling.

"You did it going up."

"Yea, but I wasn't looking down."

"Well don't look down now. Hang on to the rope, keep your feet on the side of the wall and slide slowly down to me."

"Here goes."

Cecily was more nimble than she thought she was and edged nicely over the rock and very slowly made a five foot descent. Rainbird caught her butt. Even in this treacherous moment his first thought was of how soft and round it felt.

"Okay, now we do it again," he said. "Five more feet."

Rainbird started down. When it was Cecily's turn as she grabbed the rope, her hand slid right out of his huge glove as it fell to the ground below. The rope burn surprised her and as she grabbed for a rock hold, she missed. She dangled by one hand, Rainbird stepped back up, grabbed her feet one at a time and placed them on his shoulders.

"Cecily, I'm holding on okay. I"m going to hand you the end of the rope. I want you with one hand to tie it around yourself wherever you can, under your arms or around your waist or through your harness or someplace. When I know you're secure I can look around for a good foothold and figure out the next step"

With her bleeding rope-burned hand Cecily grabbed the rope, fed it through a loop on her harness tied a tenuous knot, and though she was dangling still, Rainbird was relieved of her full weight.

Then, as Cecily looked up she heard a loud thump. She looked down. Rainbird was gone. He hadn't even called. He must be hurt. She would have to do this alone, and fast. She had to get to him and get help. If she loosened the knot she had tied in the rope she could slide down a little further. When she was as low as she could go she would jump. It was the only way.

When she reached the end of the rope, Cecily looked down again. About twelve feet it looked like, but she couldn't see Rainbird down there. "Get ready, get set, go," she said to no one as she pushed outward from the rock with her feet and let go of the rope at the same time. She flew through the air and landed in a squat but safely on her feet and rolled over onto the mushy mud on the edge of the brook. She caught her breath but couldn't take the time to check out her bones. She had to find Rainbird. She saw him almost immediately, just a few feet away from her but with his head downward, the water of the brook washing partly over his face but sparing his nose. He was breathing. He had probably been saved from drowning by landing on his backpack.

"Rainbird, Rainbird," she was crying as she called desperately. She put her arm under his neck to raise his head slightly out of the water and toward herself.

He opened his eyes. "What happened?"

"You fell from the rock when you were trying to rescue me. I'm calling 911. Don't move in case you hurt your spine. I'll keep your head above the water."

"I think I'm okay. You don't have to call 911 Cecily until I try to move and see if anything's wrong." He rotated one shoulder at a time, lifting the arm, bending his elbow, and stretching his fingers. "Okay," he said smiling up at her.
He rotated one ankle at a time. "They still work, see?" Then he bent one knee at a time. "Can't break this old goat. See? Don't know if I can get up though."

"Rainbow, I'll support your head while you roll onto your side. Then we can sit you up from there."

"I'm so sorry," Cecily cried as she sat beside Nicco when they had gotten him to a sitting position.

"Cecily, don't. It's not your fault and you can see I'll be fine. Probably a little concussion. I'd rather be here with you than anyplace else I can think of. And don't worry, I haven't lost my memory of the day's events. No siree. Haven't forgotten a thing except my fall from the rock. Don't remember how that happened."

Cecily went to the truck and brought it up closer. If you can stand and get in, I'm driving back," she said. "And you are going to the emergency room. I want to be sure nothing's broken and nothing inside's bleeding." She helped him stagger to the truck and put blankets around him in the passenger seat.

Nicco looked so terrible that when they arrived at the emergency room he was seen and examined immediately. The emergency room report was good. Lots of bruises and a few gashes on his face, ears. He was released after scans and x-rays showed nothing broken, nothing askew. Cecily called her parents from the emergency room to report the good/bad news.

When they arrived back at Rainbird's house her parents were there waiting. By that time the bruises were big and purple on both cheek bones, he had bandaging over one ear, his hair was still wet. Both of them wore soaked, dirty and torn clothes and had, what looked like, lots of mosquito bites all over their arms. Wally just shook his head. "With the way you look, it's hard to believe that you're okay," he said.

Cecily and Rainbird smiled to each other and Wally shook his head, when Evelyn said, "I brought some chicken soup over for you."

"I think Rainbird needs to lie down now," Cecily said. She took him into the bedroom, sat him on the bed, took off his shoes, fluffed his pillow, helped him lie down, pulled off his jeans and pulled the blanket over him. Then she returned to the kitchen and ate some of her mother's chicken soup.

After recounting some of their day's experiences she thanked her dad for caring for the animals so that they could have a day in the mountains. "It was a wonderful day, Dad, despite how it ended," she said. "I'll be staying here tonight in case Rainbird needs me."

Cecily showered and found one of Rainbird's tees to sleep in. She had to remove the mud-soaked clothes she was wearing. Rainbird had only one bed but she was able to climb in behind him without awakening him. In the morning she awoke first, put on the coffee and taped a note to the toilet lid, *"I'm out feeding the animals. You stay put. You shouldn't be working right after a concussion. I'll bring in some fresh eggs and poach them for you."*

About noon Wally arrived with a suitcase full of Cecily's things. Her mother had cleaned the top of her dresser, put everything into the overnight case and handed it to Wally saying, "We don't want Cecily to think we're happy to get rid of her so be sure you invite them for dinner."

Cecily declined dinner though. "I think Nicco doesn't need any excitement right now," she said. Though in truth she was concerned about Nicco, she was tickled to be settling into his home with her own things. This would be home now. Finally, Cecily was home. Both Rainbird and Cecily ached from head to toe as if they had been on a battle front, after their rock-climbing expedition, but they were able to cuddle and tuck into each other until falling asleep.

"I've wanted you my whole life," Nicco said to her, on their third night together. "When we were kids, you were more like my idol. Then you left and I tried to forget you, but every now and then you'd turn up, something would remind me of you and I would dream of you again. When you were with Aubrey, I thought I'd lost you. I never dreamt you would be able to love me as I love you."

"You are so beautiful," she said gazing at him, "You're everything I've hoped for. But Rainbird, I am a fallen woman. It's not just my teenage pregnancy that I'm thinking of. I'm pretty much over that now, but I've hurt my parents so badly, I've never been able to get very close to anyone, even my fiancé' who needed me…"

"Cecily try not to think now about all those things you have or haven't done. Think of all the time we will have together, all the time we need to learn about the best and worst of each other."

He chuckled, his brown, almost black eyes full of mirth. "Cecily, You're a fool. We all have some brokenness you know. You'd be awfully boring if you were perfect… like me." He laughed again. "For Pete's sake, don't try to be perfect. You are an independent, capable caring woman whom I have always loved because of who you are, not because of what has transpired over the years. You blend my wonderful childhood with the best me that I can be now. You have made me feel worthwhile in my simple contribution to this world.

Cecily waited two weeks until she felt sure Rainbird had recovered completely, and then, much too soon, She and Romeo were jumping into her truck for their trek back to Seaside.

"I should never have let us get this close," she said as she was getting ready to leave.

"What do you mean? Cecily nothing will separate us now. Only you can decide what to do about your business in Oregon. But I can at least wait for you now. I can know that whatever you have to give, you will give it to me. Ceci, I will help you. Don't ever again feel disconnected or ashamed."

Chapter 24

Romeo

2021

Romeo died in his sleep. He was thirteen years old, very old for a Dobie. Cecily had been taking him in to work with her now that her office and home were in the same warehouse and when they were at home he spent most of his time by the fireplace that she had had installed in her warehouse home, just for Romeo. Then one morning she found him lying still, on his big bed there by the fireside. She had never perceived that he was sick or in pain, just slow and dignified. She collapsed onto his bed next to his cold body, trying to somehow create another hour to be with him. When the hour was past, she loaded up her truck, wrapped him up in his bomber jacket, struggled to lift him bed and all into the bed of the truck and left for Oklahoma.

She headed first to her parents' home so that she and her dad, who loved Romeo so, could cry together.

"God, I'm a slow learner," she cried to her dad. "All these things that have happened to me and I never faced the truth. It took Romeo's death to teach me. I could have moved here a couple of years sooner and let him run around the farm and have you to love him. But no, I had to drag him back and forth and live in a warehouse with him, and just keep missing you and Mom and Rainbird. It's time for me to dump the illusion that I'm important to my work or that it is so important to me.

"I can't do it anymore. I can't face life all by myself. What took me so long,? It took Romeo's death to make me believe the truth?"

"There, there," Wally said as he patted her shoulder.

"My education was supposed to prepare me, not just for a certain job, but for life and life is with the people I love." She was sobbing, "I love you so much that it hurts."

"I know you do," Wally said.

"Cecily, your mother and I discussed having a burial place for Romeo here on our farm. If you wish, we can put him back under the willow tree where our son is buried. It's been many years since we lost him, but we still grieve him. You will be grieving Romeo for a long time too. Maybe it's not all that different. He has been your whole life until now. We hope that after we're gone, you will want to keep this farm. You'll always have a way to remember him if his burial place is here."

"I would love to bury him here, if it's okay. But don't you go talking about when you and Mom are gone. I can't bare that right now."

And so Rainbird dug a hole and they buried Romeo, not next to baby Jake but across on the other side of the tree. Maybe it could be the beginning of a future pet cemetery, for Cecily knew that in no time she would find another dog that would fill her up with giggles and such joy, that she would just have to rescue it.

Chapter 25

The Beginning

2021

Cecily settled back into Rainbird's home and after she did, she drove to town, determined to find some kind of job here in Broken Bow so that she could really and permanently make the move to Broken Bow. Maybe she could come full circle and become a dime store clerk again. What else could Broken Bow offer to a person whose whole career had been building businesses that had no use in a small town like Broken Bow, Oklahoma?

Well she did find an opening in the "Home Again Real Estate Company". She would be working on commission again and would probably be someone else's gopher most of the time until she obtained an Oklahoma license. But it was something, a beginning. She had a goal to work toward and with her experience she would soon be on her own. Who knows, if things worked out here she might be the owner of the business in no time. Broken Bow could be on the growing edge of tourism with good advertising and a lot of creativity.

Her parents and Nicco were thrilled with her decision to sell the Oregon businesses. It would not take long to sell them as both of them had staff who were willing, able to obtain loans and ready to purchase the businesses. She had hired and taught her staff well.

Cecily did do well at "Home Again" in Broken Bow, but when offered the manager position a year later she again took stock of her possibilities.

"Nicco was painting the window frames on his own house when she drove up to the house that day, home from work at the agency. He jumped down from the ladder and kissed her on the mouth, carefully holding his wet paint splattered hands out to the side looking like a great white heron in light. "How's it look?" he asked. "Just have to finish this window and I'll be in. Don't do any cooking til I get there. We have to celebrate."

"What are we celebrating?" Cecily asked.

"You," he answered.

"Did you know? That Marley offered me the manager position at work," she said proudly after her kiss. "Trouble is, it will take more regular hours and more responsibility, and I might be bringing work home if I take the job."

Rainbird didn't want her to see that he was immediately crest fallen so recovered quickly.

"Cecily, do what makes you feel most fulfilled, most happy," Rainbird said.
"We are doing fine, financially. You don't have to keep your job to support me and the animals. There is plenty of work to do around here if you want to be an animal junkie like me instead of working in town.

"And don't forget, you promised Jahanara that she can stay the whole summer with you this year.

"But then, if you love your job, you must advance to manager. You have too many ideas to let them brew forever, while you run errands and somebody else runs the show around the office. And then you come home and pester me instead with your ideas."

"Rainbird,, you are so full of wisdom, Cecily said. "I've been thinking long and hard about this job, even before I was offered this advancement today.

"I know I'm ready now to give up climbing the real estate ladder, any ladder.

"Unless of course, you need me to climb this ladder." She reached over and shook the ladder he had just descended. "I wouldn't mind climbing up there to clean our gutters or paint our house."

"Well, then we really have something to celebrate tonight."

He started back up the ladder with paint brush and the gallon can of white paint in his hands. Then she called up to him as he was climbing, "If I quit work, will you marry me Rainbird?"

And he totally forgot that he was covered with wet paint and holding a wet brush and open paint can when he jumped back down, grabbed her and whirled her in a full circle pirouette, her feet flying outward to the wind.

This book is available on Amazon.com

If you enjoyed reading "Flowering"
And its sequence "Cecily", (Flowering Book 2)
Watch for the third book in this series:
"JAHANARA 2013-2070", (Flowering Book 3)

Made in USA - Kendallville, IN
1129469_9798632567329